The Way The Story Ended

And other stories

Cari Lynn Vaughn

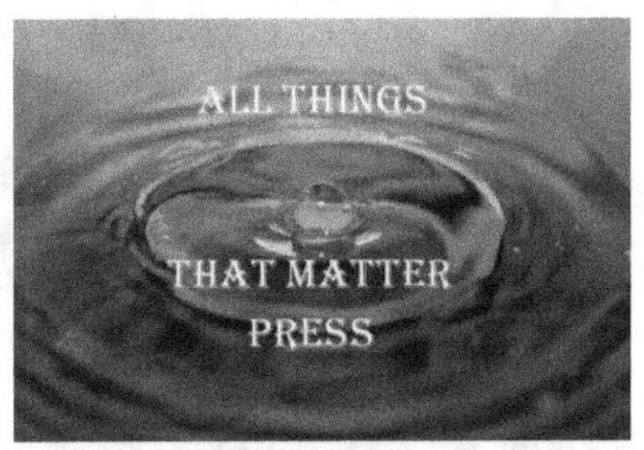

The Way The Story Ended

This is a work of fiction. Any resemblance to actual persons, living or dead, is purely coincidental.

ISBN 13: 9780988542778

Library of Congress Control Number: 2013932874

Cover design by All Things That Matter Press
Published in 2013 by All Things That Matter Press

This book is dedicated to Lance Constien and Lynne Smelser
From the Shelby Daily Globe.
Thanks for giving me my first break.

The Way the Story Ended

CHAPTER 1

Clover, Ohio Spring
Monday, March 16, 1992

She was always getting herself into dangerous situations and was reminded constantly of how un-ladylike it was, but Paige refused to change her ways. She loved pushing the envelope at her job at The Daily Clover. However, one day Paige got in way over her head.

It all started with a phone call—one out of many she'd receive before the day ended. The old phone rang four times before she stopped typing long enough to answer it.

"Hello, Paige Lynn speaking. How can I help you?"

"There's a murder that's going to take place tonight and I want *you* to be there to cover the story."

"Wouldn't it be better if I were there to stop it instead of just write about it?" she said, not taking the person on the other end of the line seriously.

"No, because you'll arrive too late and there'll be nothing you can do *but* write about it."

"What makes you so sure?"

"It doesn't matter. Just arrive at the front of the restaurant by the Black River Restaurant."

"Okay," Paige said, fumbling for a paper and pen. "Who is it that's supposed to be murdered and who's doing the dreadful deed?"

"I can't tell you any of that. Just come to the restaurant by the Black River and look around. You'll find plenty to write about it."

"Why me? Why not call the cops?"

"The cops can't do anything,"

"But," Paige started to protest, but it was too late. The man on the other end was gone.

Paige hung up and stared at the phone in disbelief. What should she do? Call the cops or just show up by alone as instructed? What had she gotten herself into this time? She jumped when the phone rang again. Paige collected herself and answered calmly.

It was her friend and co-worker Michael Tucker, who was recovering from a hangover and had stayed home, calling in to catch up on what he'd missed at work. She quickly asked if she could come over instead of talk on the phone. He agreed.

Paige turned off her computer, snagged her purse, and headed out the door of her office. She dashed past the presses and out the back to door to the small lot behind. There she slid into her blue sedan and pulled out onto the one way street. She turned left onto the Main Street of Clover, Ohio. It was a small community that remained mostly unchanged since its founding in the late 1800s. There were still brick businesses from the turn of the century lining the streets downtown, with small, quaint shops inside most of them. It wasn't until the edge of town that evidence of modern growth, like the new McDonalds and Pizza Hut, appeared. Paige drove by the Stapleton Drug Store, Henry's Haberdashery, Cook's Fine Furniture, Brewster's Accounting Firm, and a Shell gas station. After the light at the intersection, she began passing houses.

Eventually, she turned down a road that led toward the park. Paige parked in front of a split-level house and got out. She walked down the neatly trimmed sidewalk to the front door and rang the doorbell. It took a few moments, but soon the door swung open and Mike stood before her, his hair wild a mess and his face unshaven.

"Hey there, Paige." He smiled tiredly, ran his hand through his messy brown hair, and stepped aside so his friend could enter his house. "Looking good today," he commented as she walked over to the couch in the living room.

"Wish I could say the same of you."

"What do you want?"

"A favor."

He rolled his eyes as he sat on the couch and put his stocking feet up on the coffee table.

"Don't give me that *attitude,*" Paige said, putting a hand on her hip. "I just covered for you today and said you had the flu. I didn't tell our boss the reason you skipped writing about the Park Council meeting was because you'd thrown back one too many whiskeys with the war veterans you were supposed to be interviewing last night."

"Fine. What can I do for you?"

"I want to borrow your gun."

"What?"

"You heard me. I'm going undercover tonight and it may be dangerous. I'd like to have your gun on me in case I need it."

"What could be that dangerous in little ol' Clover, eh?"

"I got a call that there was a possible murder happening tonight at the Black River Restaurant."

"That place is all but closed down. Maybe someone's planning to stage a fake death in protest or a something equally stupid. In any case, you shouldn't just show up with a gun. The police need to know."

"That's just it; the guy on the phone said if I called the cops there'd be no story. I need to see what happens first. If there *is* a dead body, I promise to let the police handle it."

"How about I come with you and bring the gun instead?"

"No, I really think I'd be better off doing this alone."

He blew out a thoughtful breath before standing and walking to the closet. He opened the door and pulled out the case with his eight millimeter in it. After loading the clip and checking that the safety was on, he held it out. "I trust you know how to use one of these."

"I've shot one a couple of times," she said, sticking the gun in her purse.

"Be very careful."

"Of course I will," she assured him with a smile. "Now, go back to bed. I'm going home to freshen up a bit before I make my appearance at the Black River Restaurant."

Michael made a face and closed the closet door. He went back to the couch and put his feet back up. "Can't go back to sleep now. Guess I'll catch up on some baseball or something." He took the remote from the coffee table and clicked the TV on.

"Oh, and in case you were wondering, you didn't miss anything special at work today—other than my mysterious phone call."

"Cool. Who covered the meeting?"

"I did."

"Thanks," he said, flipping channels.

"No problem. I'll just let myself out."

Michael waved as she headed back toward the door. She let herself out, went back to her car, and drove to her apartment on Third Avenue. The apartment was tiny, but it was enough for just her. She didn't have any roommates, a boyfriend, a husband, or kids to worry about. Just out of college, she hadn't had any serious relationships. She hoped that one day she'd be married and out of the small town she'd grown up in. But for now, her life was Clover and the paper.

Paige parked in her normal spot, and checked her mailbox before going inside. She set her purse down, sat on her desk and flipped through her mail for the day. Bill. Bill. Credit card advertisement. News ad. Oh, there was a letter from National Geographic, rejecting her application to work for them. With a sigh, she turned her computer on and sat. She did a little typing and answered a few personal emails before leaving her desk to take a shower. After, she pulled on a pair of jeans and a T-shirt and made her way to the mini-kitchen to throw a Lean Cuisine dinner in the microwave.

She turned on her small TV set and scrolled through channels until she heard the microwave beep. Food in hand, she sat back on the couch to eat. There wasn't anything good on, so Paige's thoughts wandered to the phone call earlier that day. Who was being set up to be murdered and why? Was it some dirty politician or a criminal? There were so many questions and so few answers.

When she took her empty food container into the kitchen, she passed by her bulletin board and noticed a piece of paper tacked up to remind her that she had an appointment with Alex Bennington. Mad at herself for forgetting, Paige hastily pulled herself together and ran out the door.

Paige arrived at Alex's office where, upon entering, she set up her small tape recorder. He rambled on about starting a new business in the area and how he felt welcomed in the community. It was a fluff piece, but the kind of thing readers ate up. Less than a half an hour later she was driving down the road to the Black River Restaurant. It was dark by the time she positioned herself in the dim alley between the old barbershop and the window of the restaurant. She waited restlessly for someone, anyone, to park and go inside, but no one did.

A cat leapt out from nowhere, startling her. Her heart thumped, and she realized she was edgy.

When she heard footsteps, she peered around the corner and watched as two men met in front of the restaurant.

"It's time to settle some business," a deep voice announced.

"Yes, I agree," the other man said.

Paige tried to see who it was, but she could only see the shadowy forms of two figures at the end of the alleyway. Quietly, she moved closer until she could make out a handsome middle-aged man and another man standing near him. One was tall and thin, while the other was short and a little heavier. They continued talking, unaware that Paige was watching and listening.

"I told you that I wouldn't pay the fifty grand, but you persist."

"I need the money you promised me."

"Promised? What exactly did I promise? Now listen here, Bob, I'm sorry, but you're becoming too much of a nuisance. I'm going to have to eliminate you."

"You won't get away with it, Jack, I swear."

"I think that's where you're wrong. No one knows we're here and no one else knows about our little deal. And no one in this two-bit town would believe that Jack Noland would shoot anyone."

"Isn't there another way? I swear, I'll do anything," Bob begged. "You have my word."

"Save your whining for God," the deep voice said. There was a few seconds of silence and then a small, muffled popping sound followed by the sounds of one man slumping to the ground and the other's footsteps walking away.

It was a long time before Paige dared to emerge from the shadows. She stepped out, trying not to make any noise, in case the killer was still lurking around. Fear filled her as she crept ever closer to the limp body on the sidewalk. She bent down to examine the body. The man lay perfectly still on pavement, like a child's doll carelessly tossed aside. The man, Bob, had short blond hair, a mustache, and was dressed in a business suit. There was a blood stain above his left pocket; it was spreading out over his chest. He face was frozen in a painful grimace. Paige noticed a red scarf on the floor that looked like it belonged to a fortuneteller or belly dancer. She picked it up and stuffed it in her pocket. A light flipped on above the dark restaurant. Time to make her exit before someone came outside to investigate.

CHAPTER 2

That night Paige was restless, images of the murder hanging in her head. She assumed it had been reported to the police, but didn't know for sure. She was the only witness, but she had the sinking feeling no one would believe her. And, if she printed a story about the murder, the police would wonder why she hadn't come forward to make a report. If she made a report, then whatever evidence her tipster wanted her to bring to light might be lost. She had no idea what her next move should be.

Frustrated, Paige got up, took a sleeping pill, and crawled back into bed. As she drifted to sleep, she decided to return to the scene of the crime in the morning before work and then check to see what the police had come up with before writing her story.

***

Groggy and still in a daze, she got ready for work, and drank two cups of coffee in an attempt to herself to face the day. Since she was running late, she had no time to return to the Black River Restaurant before work; that would have to wait until either lunch or the end of the day. Eager, though, Paige started to draft an article. It would not be submitted until she did a little more legwork and fact-checked some things.

Mike came up behind her as she typed with great focus. "Must be some story," he said looking over her shoulder.

"It is," she muttered without looking up.

"Mind telling me what's so urgent that you don't have the time to pay attention to me?"

"Aw, are your feelings hurt?" she teased as she turned around in her swivel chair.

"Yeah, they are," he said, sticking his bottom lip out.

"Don't you have work of your own to do?"

"Yes, I do, but I swung by to ask if you wanted me tag along to take pictures of the wedding at Sacred Heart tomorrow or not."

"Yes, my hands are full and I'll need all the help I can get."

"Ooh, sounds exciting. Have a new boyfriend or something? Don't tell me you're dating the president of Thorn-Corp."

Paige screwed up her face in disgust, "Yeah, like I'd date someone with a rep for hitting on anything and everything that moves."

Mike grinned. "Gotta start somewhere."

"Humph. If I wanted to start at the bottom of the food chain, I would have dated *you*."

Mike put his hand over his heart. "Ouch. That hurt. Fine, I'll leave you to your Pulitzer-Prize winning story."

"Thanks," she said, turning back around. She finished her first draft and printed it out before reporting to Scott with the story due that day and the new one she was working on.

Scott's office was in the back of the newsroom, with a window looking down onto the printing presses. It was cramped and cluttered, and over the past hundred years-plus that the paper had been in business, ink from the presses had stained everything.

Paige tapped on the old wooden door, unable to see through the frosted glass window. "Come in," Scott called. She entered and handed him the two stories she was working on. Scott looked up from the proofs he was reviewing and took the pages from her hands. He was a high strung guy with the permanent wrinkled forehead to prove it.

"The second story is something that wasn't assigned, but if you read it, I'm sure you'll want to run it," she said.

Scott skipped to the second article and skimmed it. "Seriously?" he said when he'd finished.

"Yeah, seriously. I really did get a phone call yesterday. And when I went to the restaurant, I heard a shot and saw the dead body."

"Paige, I do believe you've gotten yourself in over your head this time. Does anyone else know?"

"Not yet."

"You know we have to call the police and report this before we can run it."

"I'm sure they already know. And if they don't, they'll find out when we run the story tomorrow."

"Just back up your facts at the very least so we don't get sued. Okay?"

"Fine." She turned to leave and go back to her desk, but stopped as Scott spoke again.

"You do realize the killer could very well come after you for being an unwanted witness. You could be putting yourself in grave danger if we print this article."

"Well, I had hoped the police would launch an investigation into Jack Noland and that I wouldn't have to worry about it. But I suppose you do have a point. Even he doesn't come after me in person, he could send someone to do his dirty work for him."

"That's why you need to be careful."

"So you'll print the story?"

"If you do some fact-checking first and cover your ass."

"Thanks!" Paige smiled and, as Scott shook his head, disappeared out the door.

Paige sat her desk and began working on editing several pieces and arranging interviews for some more assignments. She was buried in work when the phone rang once again. Expecting it to be a returned phone call from someone she hadn't been able to reach earlier in the day, she was surprised. It was her very own mysterious deep throat calling to follow up about the murder.

"Miss Lynn?"

"Speaking."

"Did you go last night?"

"You mean the Black River Restaurant? Yeah, I was there."

"Did you see what happened?"

"Yeah, I heard Bob get shot."

"And are you going to write about it?"

"Already have, but I need to call the police before we can go ahead and print it."

"Don't do that."

"Why not?"

"Because he's paying off the police."

"He who?"

"The one who shot Bob. Did you catch his name?"

"Yeah, Jack Noland announced who he was right before he shot him."

"And you don't know who Jack is?"

"The name rings a bell, but I can't quite place him."

"He's only the most powerful man in all of Clover. Perhaps you *do* need to do some more research before you print."

"And who are you? Why are you blowing the whistle on this guy?"

"Doesn't matter."The line went dead.

"Damn it."

After a moment, Paige picked the phone back up and dialed the Clover Police Department. She spoke to Barb the dispatcher and asked about anything unusual that might have taken place the night before.

"Just your usual DUIs, domestic violence and traffic violations. What were you looking for something in particular?"

"No murders?"

Barb snorted. "There hasn't been a murder in Clover in quite a few years."

"Maybe that's because they all go to Pottersfield to die," Paige said as she laughed. Pottersfield, the next town over, had a reputation for being a poor place to live. Drugs and gang-related shootings made for a great deal of violence in the city. Clover, by comparison, was trapped in the 1950s—at least, that was picture the mayor wanted painted of the city. Certainly, Clover had its own dark underbelly no one wanted to talk about. Bob's death was proof of that.

"No shootings then or John Does at the morgue?"

"Not that I'm aware of."

"Anything happen at the Black River Restaurant?"

"No reports of anything. Why? You know something?"

"Nah, just fishing. I'll talk to you later. Thanks. Bye," Paige said quickly, wanting to dodge talking about what she'd witnessed.

Time to do some digging on Jack Noland. Paige ran a search for all articles about him and then checked the public records. Before she had to leave for an interview, she had a much better idea of who he was:

Jack Ryan Noland was born in Memphis, Tennessee in 1947 to Donna and Donald Noland. Donald migrated from Memphis to

Pottersfield to work at the Steel factory in the 1950s. They moved to Clover in 1962 when Donald Noland got a promotion. Jack attended Centennial High School from 1961 until 1964. He graduated with honors and went on to attend Ohio State University, where he graduated with an MBA in 1970. He moved back to Clover in 1972 and began working at Thorn-Corp and soon purchased AJP Insurance as well. He married Janet Deville in 1971 and they had two kids: Joan, born in 1973, and Jennifer in 1976. He divorced Janet in 1983 and married a younger woman named Nicole Barnhart. They had a son together, Jack Jr., born in 1983 as well. Jack had no criminal record and was not publically linked to any organized crime. The only thing that stood out was ties to a railroad company in Cleveland, but that was inconclusive, at best.

Articles started to appear about him in the late eighties as he climbed the corporate ladder and began to buy up properties around Clover. He owned nearly half the town, but remained largely a silent partner in most businesses. A baseball field had been named after him most recently. That fact made her jerk in her seat. That was why his name was familiar; she'd written about the dedication of the new field.

CHAPTER 3

Tuesday, March 17, 1992

Once she finished her turkey sandwich lunch, Paige hopped in her car and went over to the high school to interview Hunter Douglas, a teacher who was running for mayor in the next election.

"What made you decide to go into politics" was the obvious question on everyone's mind.

"I've been a member of the School Board for nearly ten years now and I've been teaching here at Centennial High School for fifteen years. There are always a lot of politics involved, so I don't think being mayor will be that much different than the sort of job I've been dong for years. I feel like I have an idea of what the needs of the community here in Clover are. I know most of the parents and their children at this point, so that makes it easier to trust me," Mr. Douglas answered as if he'd rehearsed the answer a million times before she'd arrived. "I am familiar," he added.

"What changes do you hope to introduce into the community if you are elected mayor?"

"I'd like to work on getting more government funding to the arts and make sure that we don't have to give up our wonderful music and theater programs at Centennial. I would like to see some of the old buildings either knocked down or restored, depending on the state of the building and the costs involved. Clover is a beautiful town and I would like others to see it as I do."

"In past years the famous Fourth of July fireworks have been canceled due to lack of funding and complaints about the noise disturbance downtown during the festival. Do you have plans to reinstate any sort of festival?"

Mr. Douglas smiled. "Glad you asked. As a matter of fact, I've been researching our options and I think I found a way to make everyone happy. While there will no longer be a beer garden, we can still close down one of the main streets and have some vendors and rides. It won't be as big, but it would be something at least.

Furthermore, I think we can solve the budge issue by having the fireworks a week after the Fourth. We can purchase fireworks at a discount and celebrate our town's heritage at the same time. Clover is famous for its manufacturing of bicycles in the 1950s, so we could hold a celebration in honor of those golden days."

"So instead of the Fourth of July, we'll have Bicycle Days? "I know a lot of people have missed the summer celebration downtown since they stopped having it few years ago—including me."

"Yeah, I think it would be the best way to make everybody happy. The Shelby Cycle Company manufactured bicycles in Clover, Ohio from nineteen twenty-five to nineteen fifty-three. Their bikes are popular among collectors for their styling. They produced a bicycle in nineteen twenty-eight with a Charles Lindbergh theme called the 'Lindy Flyer', and they were responsible for the Donald Duck bicycles in the nineteen fifties. Clover also made bicycles for other retailers such as Montgomery Ward, Spiegel, Gambles stores, Firestone and Goodyear. AMF purchased Clover in nineteen fifty-three. A separate company, called The Clover Bicycle Company, manufactured the Ideal Bicycle from eighteen ninety-five until around nineteen-o-one to nineteen-o-two."

"I did not know that," Paige said. She'd grown up in Clover, but all she remembered of AMF was an empty parking lot that she learned to drive in.

They chatted a bit longer and then Paige excused herself, saying she had other obligations. She thanked Hunter Douglas for his time. She wanted to return to The Black River Restaurant before dark. She drove down the narrow one-way street and parked in front of the old building. The restaurant was closed even though it normally would have been ideal hours for dinner customers. Paige got out of her car and looked at the spot where she'd seen Bob's body. There was no chalk outline and no blood. More importantly, there was no body, either.

"Strange," Paige muttered, bending down and looking all over the broken slate sidewalk for clues. It seemed someone had disposed of the body before the police could be called. If Paige ran her story now, she'd look like a liar. A man had been shot; she'd heard it. And he'd been lying on the sidewalk, dead; she'd seen it. Well, she'd seen that he was at least unconscious and bleeding. There was the remote possibility that Bob got up and walked away, but Paige didn't think that was the case.

Curious, she went to the door to the apartment up above the restaurant and rang the bell. A few minutes later, an old gentleman answered.

"I was wondering if you heard any commotion or saw anything out of the ordinary in front of your restaurant last night."

The old man shook his head no.

"No cars backfiring?" She knew if she said "gunshots" he'd clam up.

He shook his head no again.

Paige dug out one of her cards. "Well, if you happen to remember anything, please give me a call."

He took the card and nodded yes before shutting the door in her face.

"Thanks," she murmured at the closed door. Paige turned and walked back to her car completely confused. Was the owner of the restaurant one of the men who helped dispose of the body, she wondered, or maybe got Bob medical attention?

Paige looked at her watch and realized she'd promised to meet Mike for drinks at Reece's Bar and Grill. She drove onto Main Street and up past Clover Avenue to the old bar uptown. The cozy bar with its old-fashioned wood paneled walls had been there since the early 1900s, but the name and type of food served with the drinks had changed over the years. The giant mirror inside its carved wooden frame was an elegant sight. Too bad it came complete with TVs on the shelves for customers to keep up with the latest news and sports. That killed the ambiance, in Paige's opinion.

Mike was sitting in a corner booth back by the kitchen when she arrived. She slid into the seat next him and watched as he took a swig from his green Heineken bottle. "Run into anymore problems, kid," he asked affectionately.

"Just the total absence of proof any crime was ever committed."

A waitress named Sookie came over and took Paige's order. She asked for a Heineken and a burger, which was the exact same thing Mike had ordered five minutes before she'd arrived. Sookie disappeared and Mike asked Paige what she meant.

"I went back to the scene of the crime and there was no body and no evidence of any foul play. The restaurant owner and the police say nothing out of the ordinary happened last night, but I *know* what I saw. I'm *not* crazy."

Mike took another drink of beer. "Well, you are crazy, you know, but I don't think you hallucinated the whole thing. I believe you when you say something happened."

"Thanks." She paused and added, "I think."

Mike laughed as Sookie set a beer down in front of Paige and opened it. "So are you going to run the story still?"

"If Scott will let me. He told me to check my contacts and I did. They just don't add up to what I saw."

"Well, maybe you can run it as a sort of editorial or something."

Paige took a long drink and said, "Or something."

Soon their burgers came and they started talking about other things like the Cleveland Indians. The conversation drifted to tales of being drunk and disorderly, among other things, before Paige decided to leave.

"Ah, so soon," a half-drunk Mike whined as she tossed money on the table. He was on his third or fourth beer by then. Paige had lost count. It could have been more.

"Yeah, so soon. I'm tired and I still have to revise my article so I can print it tomorrow. See you at work," she said leaning over and kissing him on the cheek.

He smiled.

Paige left the bar and went back to her car, her mind reeling. What was she going to say? How could she write a brilliant article that wouldn't make her look like a liar or a fool? And how was she going to get it into Scott before printing time?

CHAPTER 4

And Then There Were None

By Paige Lynn

I am writing this as a plea to anyone who might have more details about what happened on the night of Monday, March 16, 1992.

In the morning of that date, I received an anonymous phone call advising there was going to be a murder at the Black River Restaurant. I was told to show up and write about what I saw, but not to call the police. Once there, I heard an argument between two men from my spot in the alley. One was named Bob and the other identified himself as local businessman Jack Noland. I heard a gunshot and rushed out to see what happened. Bob lay bleeding on the sidewalk.

He looked to be dead. When I saw the light come on upstairs above the restaurant, I was sure the cops were on their way. Imagine my surprise when I found out there was no body and no crime reported. I received a second anonymous phone call begging me to write about what I saw, but my editor is hesitant to print a piece that I could not back up with facts. Again, if anyone has any information, please contact me.

Thank you. Paigelynn@clover.ap.us

Paige turned the piece in, hoping Scott wouldn't read it and reject it. There was a chance he'd miss it, late as it was, or perhaps skim it, but not read closely enough to see she still didn't have any facts to back up her story.

As she drove home at just before midnight, Paige realized how exhausted she was. But when she opened her door, adrenaline rushed through her body. Her apartment had been ransacked.

Paige put things back where they belonged and made sure nothing was missing. No money had been stolen and she had no jewelry worth anything. Whoever had been in her apartment had tossed all her CDs and videos to the floor, but had not removed any. She decided it was a warning to stop digging up info on Jack Noland and nothing more. Paige decided not to call the police.

***

She awoke the next morning to the insistent ringing of her telephone. Still feeling tired, she pulled herself out of bed and dragged herself to the kitchen to answer it. "Hello," she finally said.

It was Scott and he was not happy. "Paige Lynn, you are to get your ass down here *now.*"

"Why? It's only six in the morning. Did something happen?"

"Yes, now get down here."

"I'll be in as soon as I can," she said, yawning.

"That better be less than a half an hour."

"Something like that," she grumbled as she hung up the phone.

When she entered Scott's office, he told her to shut the door and handed her a piece of paper. It was a typewritten statement, signed in black ink.

Jack Noland was at home with his wife and son the night of Monday, March 16, 1992. They are his witnesses and are willing to swear to this in a court of law. He never has been and never will be involved in any illegal activity. Mr. Noland is deeply shocked and wounded by the article in which Ms. Lynn accuses him of murder, and is considering taking legal action against Ms. Lynn and the Daily Clover for libel. We suggest that Ms. Lynn be fired immediately and a retraction with full apology be printed in tomorrow's newspaper.

Sincerely,
Anne-Marie Poulton, Administrative Assistant to Mr. Jack Noland.

"I don't know what to say," Paige said.

Scott, jaw clenched, said, "You can say goodbye, because you are being fired immediately after writing that letter of apology so that we do not get our asses sued. This paper cannot afford to pay out the sort of damages that Jack Noland is going to demand if this goes to court."

"But you printed the article."

"Without my knowledge. I told you to get your facts straight and make sure you had proof before we went to print, which you failed to do. It was irresponsible of you to print such unsubstantiated claims without proper proof."

"But I know what I saw. A man claiming to be Jack Noland shot Bob. I just want to know what happened that night."

Scott winced, buried his head in his hands and then looked up, exasperated, turning both palms up in plea. "A man *claiming* to be Jack Noland? Do you realize what bullshit we've printed? Why didn't you leave this one alone? Haven't you ever heard the saying 'curiosity killed the cat'?"

"Well, yeah, but isn't it our job as journalists to be curious? To ask the hard questions?"

"As a small town newspaper, we are here to report what readers want to know. We're here to celebrate someone's son scoring the winning touchdown at the football game. We're here to celebrate who was crowned Prom King and Queen. We are *not* here to investigate crimes or point out the flaws of this small community."

Paige folded her arms and widened her stance. "Corruption and murder should be newsworthy no matter if they happen in a small town or big city."

"Our readers are blissfully unaware of the few unpleasant incidents that have occurred over the years and they will remain that way. I guarantee we'll lose a large portion of our readership if we start focusing on all the negative crap that goes on around here."

"Like the teenager whose death was ruled an accident when many of his friends knew it was a drug-related murder? Or like the drowning death of another teenager, also ruled an accident when everybody knew it was suicide?"

"Yes. The people of Clover do not want to feel like their community is unsafe. Kids killing each other, or themselves, makes everyone uncomfortable. We don't need to add to the bleakness of the world we live in today."

"Yeah, that's what the evening news is for."

"Well, then go get a job with TV 78. You are free to work wherever you want now."

"Nobody watches TV 78. And it isn't even out of Clover, but out of Pottersfield. You know as well as I do that I'd have to move to Cleveland, Columbus, Cincinnati or Toledo to cover any real news. And all of those cities are an hour drive or more away from here."

Scott snorted. "Maybe this is your chance to move out of this town, then."

Paige was silent for a moment before she said, "I just don't think this is fair. I didn't actually accuse anyone of murder. I just stated the facts as I saw them. It was a plea for someone to come forward with the truth. I wasn't trying to libel anyone."

Scott sighed. "I know that and you know that, but apparently Jack Noland doesn't. And what you wrote *is* libelous. Legally, my hands are tied. Maybe after this all blows over, we can work something out but, for now, you no longer work at The Daily Clover."

"Fine," Paige said, close to tears of anger. She turned and went to clean out her desk.

"What happened," Mike asked coming up behind Paige as she threw her pictures, notes, and other personal belongings into an empty box.

"Scott fired me," Paige said throwing her MTD mug, still filled with pens, into the box. One of the pens was leaking and got ink all over her hand, but she didn't care.

"He can't do that."

"He can. He did."

"What for?"

"That stupid piece I wrote about the murder."

"Oh." Mike nodded in understanding.

"Jack Noland is really pissed."

Mike smiled.

"What? That isn't funny."

"No, it isn't funny. You've gone and stirred up a hornet's nest. But you still may be onto something."

"Well, I keep telling you, I know what I saw and what I heard."

"Look, why don't you go home and get some rest? You look like you could use it. Let me see what I can dig up for as far as proof goes. Okay?"

"Could you? Oh, that would be wonderful, Mike. I'd really owe you."

"You could just date me and we'd call it even."

"Um, no," Paige said shaking her head. "We've been over this before."

"I know, but since we're no longer co-workers ...."

"Still no." Paige grinned. "But I do love you."

***

Paige was carrying her box and leaving, when Scott called out, "And don't forget the apology."

"Crap," she said as she turned around. She went back to her desk, turned on the computer and typed her last words for The Daily Clover.

It is with deepest regret that I leave the staff of The Daily Clover. I am truly sorry if I have offended Mr. Jack Noland in any way. It was not my intention to soil his good name, but to call out the truth from the public. I was witness to something that night, but I can't say who it was for sure. I was depending on someone from the community to come forward and fill in the blanks. My piece should not have been published until it was properly proven. I do not bear any ill will toward Mr. Noland or any of his family or associates. Please accept my most humble apology.

Sincerely, Paige Lynn.

Paige printed it out and dropped the single page in Scott's mail slot before heading toward the door once again. She drove home, determined to find a way to solve the mystery and get her job back.

CHAPTER 5

Wednesday, March 18, 1992

She'd been sleeping for several hours when the phone woke her again. "What now?" she said, rolling over looking up at the ceiling. The phone didn't stop ringing, so she threw off the covers and went to answer it.

"Hello."

"It's me, Mike."

"Yeah."

"There's been another murder."

"You're kidding."

"Nope, and this time it's someone you know: Rose Saint James. She was found this morning in her bathtub. At first they thought it was just an accident and that she'd just slipped and fell."

"But?"

"With her clothes on, no less. No, they found a bullet wound in her chest and that's when they couldn't deny it was a murder any longer."

"Poor Rose. She was a good friend."

"Yeah, but I have a feeling the cause of her death is going to be kept hush-hush, you know."

"You think it's related to Bob's murder?"

"That's my hunch, but I'm going to have to see if I can find any connections. Anyway, just thought you should know."

"Thanks, Mike. Call me as soon as you know anything."

"Okay," he said as they hung up.

Paige sighed. She decided it was time to clean and do some laundry while she mulled over the facts. She felt responsible somehow and was determined to put a stop to whatever it was Jack Noland was up to. The question was how could she ever hope to uncover the truth when it was costing her so much?

She was mindlessly checking her pockets before tossing her jeans into the washing machine when she pulled out a red scarf. She looked at it blankly for a moment before remembering she'd taken it from the crime scene.

It was time to call in a favor from her friend Steve at the pathology lab in Pottersville.

When she arrived, Steve was looking through a microscope at something. He stopped and glanced up at her when his assistant opened the lab door and let Paige in. She extended her hand and showed him the scarf. "I found this at a crime scene. Can you run some tests on it and see what you can find?"

Steve's eyebrows knitted. "Why don't the police have this?"

"It was, ah, overlooked. Can you do whatever you guys do here in the lab and let me know if you find anything?"

"Are we talking DNA, blood stains, or something else?"

"Yes," she smiled. "All that—everything. Test it for everything and tell me as much you can about that particular scarf. It was all that was left the crime scene. There wasn't even a dead body, so you see how important it is."

"I'll do my best, but I've got a lot of work to do here."

"That's fine. Just sometime soon."

"Will do."

"Thank you, Steve. You are a godsend."

"Well, science-send anyway." He chuckled.

"What are you working on?"

"DNA right now. I think it is going to be key in the trial against that doctor who buried his dead wife in the basement."

"Allegedly. He hasn't been convicted yet."

Steve stuck his forefinger at her with a knowing grin. "But he will be."

"Good luck."

"Thanks."

"No, thank you," Paige said, turning to leave.

She decided it was time to go to the phone company and see if she could get her phone records from the newspaper. Figuring out who her informant was would be a good place to start unraveling this mystery. Fortunately, she had a friend who worked for Sprint.

"Carol, could you do me a favor," Paige asked as they sat in the break room together.

Carol opened her Diet Coke with her long red nail and said, "Sure, what's up?"

"I received phone calls on Monday and Tuesday from the same guy. He wouldn't say who he was or where he was at, but he told me some accurate information about something bad that happened just as he said it would. I need to know who my source was, but I can't name him if I don't know who he is. I"m in a whole lot of hot water here and I need you to help me clear my name and avoid this libel suit waiting to happen."

"Of course. After I eat, we'll see what we can find."

When she'd finished, they returned to Carol's cubicle and Carol pulled up the records for the past week attached to the newspaper's various lines.

"Here we go, "Carol said after considerable searching. "Looks like a private number that belongs to one Maurice Metroff." She rattled off the address and phone number. "Anything else?"

"No, that's exactly what I need," Paige said, jotting the information in her notebook. "Thanks a bunch, Carol."

"No problem. Hope you can clear your name soon and get your job back."

"Me, too. Talk to you soon"

***

Paige found her way to the Downing Street address of Maurice Metroff's house. It was an unassuming ranch in the newer part of town. Not shabby, but not the Ritz, either. She guessed he was middle-management in one of Jack Noland's companies. Paige knocked on the door and waited for an answer.

A middle-age man with a receding line of brown hair answered. He was in his bathrobe and was unshaven. Funny, Paige thought, this is how Mike looked two days ago. Only Mike had smelled a bit better. Maurice reeked of body odor. Trying not to make a face, Paige said, "I'm looking for Maurice Metroff."

"Yeah, what do you want?"

"You contacted me about a murder that was going to take place in front of the Black River Restaurant."

"You must be that reporter, Paige Lynn."

"Yes, I am."

"Come in before anybody sees you, for chrissake. Somebody has probably already followed you here," he said sticking his head out the door and looking around.

Paige followed him in and he shut the door. The house smelled unpleasantly of mildew and cigarette smoke. "I have some questions for you," she said.

"Excuse me a minute, I have burgers on the stove," he said, disappearing through a small hallway to the kitchen.

Her stomach was churning from the stench; it was all she could do not gag.

Maurice returned and sat in a torn rocker recliner in the living room. "So how did you find me?"

"That doesn't matter. What does matter is that I got fired for running that little number in the paper and Jack Noland is threatening to sue. I need some solid proof or else this will all be for nothing, Mister Metroff."

"Hmm, doesn't surprise me that Noland struck back. Sorry. Hadn't meant to get you in trouble. I just wanted someone to know he was a dangerous man."

"Well, Jack Noland is sending that message loud and clear right now. My friend Rosa Saint James is also dead," Paige paused to look at his eyes to see if there was any reaction, "and I believe it's because of her connection to me. I want to know why you called me and what Jack Noland is up to so we can end this before more people die."

"Yes, well, I called you because I liked your spunk. There is a noticeable attitude behind your words and I appreciate it. It set you apart from the other dull reporters at the paper."

"Thank you, but that doesn't tell me why you turned Jack Noland in. How did you know about the meeting with Bob?"

"I worked for Jack Noland at Thorn-Corp. I was his accountant for years—until recently, anyway. I was told to fudge the books and not ask questions. At first I did, but then I got curious. Turns out Jack's dividing his money into some bad business, and syphoning some cash to a mistress, as well. He doesn't want anyone to know about his kept woman or his involvement in dog racing in Florida. I got greedy and decided to try and blackmail him for more money myself."

"But you just screwed yourself out of job instead."

He leveled a forefinger at her with a wink and a nod. "Exactly."

"What about Bob?"

"What about Bob? He was Jack Noland's bookie until he double-crossed him. That's why Jack arranged the back alley meeting. There was no real way to blackmail Bob, so he killed him."

"But there was no body. That's what's getting me into so much trouble. The police can't back me up on this at all. There's no evidence that anyone was shot and so there's no way to pin it on Jack Noland."

"I told you he was paying off the police. That's why no report was filed. You can't honestly believe he could get away with murder that easily unless the chief of police was on his payroll as well?"

"That means Chief Phillips is corrupt, too. Going up against him is going to be tough, for sure."

"That's why I thought if you went public with what happened before Jack could erase all the evidence, then we might have a chance, but you went and screwed that up."

"I didn't screw it up on purpose. I expected there to be a body and lots of evidence. You never said what I witnessed would need to be videotaped or something. I had no idea what to expect. If you want to blame someone, blame yourself for not being more detailed or thorough."

Maurice picked up a pack of Lucky Strikes from the end table and shook one out. He stuck it in his mouth, lit it with a near-by lighter, inhaled and blew out a cloud of smoke. "Fine, we're both in over our heads, but Noland knows someone's on to him now. I expect any day he'll show up here and whack me as well."

"Whack?" Paige laughed.

"Would you prefer I said *off me* instead?"

"No, that just sounds wrong." She laughed again.

"However you want to phrase it, I'm sure our lives are in danger now."

"How can Jack Noland be that powerful, really? I'm sure the FBI would like to know about him. They can investigate him even if the local police are corrupt. They would be our best bet."

"Jack has some powerful connections. I don't even know if the FBI can touch him."

"Unless he's working for the CIA or some other high-level government agency, I'm positive the FBI could easily get him. You sound super spooked, though."

"He's hurt and killed others before. I know what he is capable of. He is a cold-blooded murder who will stop at nothing to preserve the picture-perfect life he's created in Clover."

"Why haven't you run?"

"Where to? I have no money and I have no family. I'm fifty-six years old and I haven't done a damn thing with my life. If I can have a hand in taking Jack Noland down, then that's something at least."

"But if you get killed and he walks free, it will all be for nothing, then, won't it?"

"Now you know, too, so you can carry on even if I can't. I'm tired and I just don't care anymore. It's too much trouble to run."

Paige shook her head sadly and sat quietly for a moment. Suddenly she said, "What's Noland's end game? Do you know the names of his contacts? We have to get some proof before we move ahead with this."

Maurice drew on his cigarette and exhaled again. "He wanted to buy up the majority of properties in Clover so he could literally own the town. I don't think he had his eyes on being mayor. In fact, I think he's either using Hunter Douglas as a puppet or he plans on trying to make him one if he wins the election."

"What property does he own? What is his strategy? Do you know?"

"Jack Noland owns one of the biggest factories in town and the biggest insurance company. That alone has brought him a great deal of power. I suspect if he could control the newspaper and the mayor, he'd have it made. I know many of the City Council members are friends of his. People from the Park Board to the School Board have all been on his payroll at some point."

"Do you have access to any of the accounting books you fudged over the years?"

"No, he took those all away from me before I could steal them for evidence against him. He hired a new guy to forge things and sign things in my place. He just erased me from existence. It's like I never worked for him."

"Weird. There has to be a paper trail somewhere, somehow. I think our best bet is to break into corporate headquarters."

"And how do you plan to do that?"

"I don't know just yet, but I'll find a way. Are you willing to help?"

"Sure, why the hell not?"

"Good. Thank you, Mister Metroff. I'll be in touch as soon as I figure out our next move." Paige stood and said, "I'll show myself out."

Maurice drew on his cigarette and blew out again while waving goodbye.

CHAPTER 6

Paige glanced at her watched and remembered she was going to still meet Mike at Reece's Bar at five o'clock

As usual, Mike was sitting in the corner drinking his after-work Heineken. And once again Paige slid into the booth beside him and ordered her own beer from Sookie. "So what did you find out about Rose Saint James?"

"Your friend worked for Jack Noland as a secretary at Thorn-Corp for five years. She quit because of a sexual harassment suit that never made it to court. Rumor has it Jack Noland compensated her and got her a job down at City Hall as a clerk in Title and Tax Department. That's where she worked the past three years."

"Why would he shoot her?"

"We don't know that he was the one who shot her," Mike said with a raise of an eyebrow. "However, her computer files have mysteriously disappeared, not-so-coincidently."

"She knew Jack Noland was fudging his books, I bet. Maybe she threatened to go to Mayor Garfield with what she knew," Paige said as Sookie set her beer on the table.

"Maybe. The police are calling it a break-in, but they claim to have no suspects at the moment. Her landlord suggested it might have been one of the men he hired to do repairs."

Paige took a drink of her beer and closed her eyes for a moment.

Mike broke her concentration by saying, "Who the hell is Maurice?"

"Maurice Metroff used to work for Jack Noland. He's my Deep Throat. I ran a check on who called me and his name was the only one I didn't recognize."

"Good work. I take it you spoke to him."

"Yes, and he's willing to do what it takes to put Jack Noland away. We only have to figure out how to get some evidence against him—something that connects him to the murders."

"We need a plan." Mike as he looked away from Paige and up at the TV. The news was on..

Paige noticed that the TV on the other side of the bar was showing a re-run of The Carol Burnette Show. Though the sound was muted, she recognized it as the dumb secretary skit she'd seen a dozen times.

"I have an idea," she said as a plate of fries was set in front of her.

"I'm all ears," Mike said, turning his attention back to her.

"I need to go undercover as a temp at Thorn-Corp. I need to be a Kelly Girl or something so I can have access to all his files. Once I gain access, I can photocopy what I need and split."

"Tricky. How do purpose to pull that off? Jack Noland probably knows your name, your address, and your favorite color by now."

Paige folded her arms and said, "What's my favorite color?"

"Ah," he said, then took a drink, trying to buy himself time. He glanced over her outfit, but it was all white. "Green," he said.

"You're hopeless."

"So what's your favorite color?"

Paige took a drink of her beer. "It won't matter if Jack Noland gets to me first."

"If you mysteriously disappear or turn up dead, I would think it would draw attention to him."

"He might not care. He thinks he's invincible."

Mike drank another swig of beer.

"Tomorrow I become a temp. Here's to temps," Paige said, picking up her beer and clanking against the bottle in Mike's hand.

They finished their dinner in silence and then Paige took off to get some rest. It had been a long day and she knew she still had lots of work ahead of her.

It wasn't until she arrived at her door that she noticed she was being followed; the two men who'd visited Maurice were also paying her a visit. She was quickly trying to unlock her door when they came up behind her.

"Paige Lynn," the big burly man asked.

"Yeah," she said turning nervously. Her face was met with a fist and Paige was out cold.

***

When Paige awoke she discovered she was on the cold, dirty floor of an empty warehouse. By the looks of it, she was in the Industrial Park at the north end of town. The industrial park had been built in the early 1900s when industry was booming. Railroads, long since defunct, crisscrossed through the grid of long, large buildings in the park. Many of the enterprises had since gone out of business, leaving approximately half the complexes empty. The MTD Tractor Manufacturer was one of the few factories left, along with American Freight Shipping, Dunlap Tires and a handful of others. Paige assumed she was in one of the empty buildings.

She moaned as she became aware of the pain in her neck, shoulders and a splitting headache. Paige tried to move and get better look at her surroundings. She noticed Maurice lying on the floor beside her. There was a bullet wound in the middle of his forehead. Paige guessed she would soon join him.

"Hello there," a voice echoed in the vacant building.

Paige craned her neck to see who was there. A heavy-set man in jeans and a black t-shirt walked into view and stood above her. He had back black hair that was shaggy and falling out of place..

"Who … who are you?"

"Associate of Jack Noland. He wanted me to deliver a message to you," the man said. .

"Which would be?"

"Time to get the the hell out of his business." The man laughed.

"You going to kill me like you killed Maurice over there?"

"You're both going to perish in a tragic fire."

Paige heard the sound of liquid being dumped on the floor around her. She turned her neck and looked around and saw a tall, thin man emptying a gas over the empty wooden pallets and boxes.

"This is insane," Paige yelped. She struggled against the ropes that bound her. "Let me go and I'll never breathe a word of this to anyone, ever."

"Sure you won't."

"Killing me now will only draw more attention to Jack Noland. He needs to lay low and stop the killing spree before he's caught."

"Jack Noland is the law of the land around here and he does as he sees fit."

"This isn't the Old West. He can't just declare himself the new Sheriff in town." Paige wriggled some more as she felt the ropes loosen around her hands.

The heavy-set man shrugged as the slender one dumped the last of the gasoline over Maurice's dead body. He dropped the can and said, "Ready to go?"

"Sure thing," the man in black said as he took out a book of matches. He lit a cigarette and then dropped the match in a pool of gasoline. The two men trotted out of the warehouse as the orange and red flames began spreading throughout the building. Maurice's body was being consumed and the smell of burning flesh filled Paige's nostrils. Trying to remain calm, she worked her way out of the ropes. She stood and looked around trying to figure out how to get out of the building as fast as possible. The south and west walls were already a wall of flames. The only exit appeared to be through a small break in the circle of dumped gasoline. The spot must have been were the two men were standing before they left. Paige dodged through the intense heat and made her way to an open dock where she jumped out and ran across the street. .

Adrenalin pumping, Paige frantically yelled for help. She looked around to find a place to call 911 from, but it didn't matter, the fire must have been spotted from far away because fire trucks were on their way. Paige stayed a safe distance and watched as the men worked hard to put the fire out. A squad car arrived on the scene, spotted Paige, and decided to take her in for questioning.

Still in shock, Paige was taken to one of their small interrogation rooms and filled out a report of what had happened. Paige wasn't sure if anyone would ever believe her, or even if they did, if that, too, would be covered up. Whatever happened, she felt obligated to at least try and reveal the truth.

"So you were abducted from your home and taken to the warehouse?" Officer Cross stated after he read through what Paige had written.

"Yes."

"Why would anyone have any reason to abduct you, Miss. Lynn?"

"Because I wrote about Jack Noland in the paper."

"But you retracted what you said, essentially saying it was all made up and that you were a liar."

"That isn't what I said. What I said was that I didn't mean to accuse anyone. I was just looking for some answers."

"Which meant you didn't have the facts when you printed your little article. Why would someone abduct you if you are in the habit of printing stuff that isn't true?"

"You're twisting my words around. My article isn't on trial here. What matters is that I was knocked out, tied up and attempt made on my life. I didn't imagine that, that's for sure."

"How do we know you aren't making up more stuff to cover the fact that you killed Maurice and set the fire to cover it all up?"

"Why on earth would I kill anyone?"

"I don't know. Why don't you tell me?"

"I didn't kill anyone. This is all one big misunderstanding."

"Uh-huh," the office mocked her.

"I demand a lawyer. I'm not talking anymore."

"Only guilty people demand lawyers."

"And only asses accuse innocent people of crimes they didn't commit."

"Guess that makes you an ass," Officer Cross said leaving the room. He shut the door behind him and Paige flipped him off. How dare he turn it around on her? She was the victim here, not the perpetrator. Paige was outraged at her treatment and thankful when they finally allowed her to return home at nearly midnight.

Paige picked up her purse that she'd dropped when she was abducted and let herself in to her apartment. . Her money, keys and the gun she'd borrowed from Mike were all still inside. Despite having the gun in her possession, she didn't feel safe in her apartment any longer, so she decided to go to the only place she knew she was welcome, Mike's.

When she rang the doorbell it was one a.m. It took him forever to answer. After five minutes, the door swung open to reveal a very weary man in boxers.

"Mike, can I sleep here tonight?"

"Don't you have your own apartment," he said yawning. A woman dressed in one of Mike's dress shirts came up behind him.

"Oh, sorry to intrude," Paige said. What should she expect? She kept turning Mike down, so he was free to look elsewhere for female companionship.

"Who's this," the woman asked.

"Just a friend from the paper."

"I wouldn't have swung by so late, but after the night I've had, I just couldn't go home."

The woman wandered back inside the house and out of sight as Mike let Paige in and invited her to sit and tell him what had happened.

"After I left you at the bar, I was hit from behind and taken to a warehouse. Two of Jack Noland's men had killed Maurice—shot him in the head, doused the place with gasoline and set fire to the place. They were going to burn us both to cover up our murders."

"But you escaped," Mike said as he sat on the couch.

"Obviously. The guys can't even tie a decent knot. They definitely weren't boy scouts."

"Guess they didn't count on you waking up before your final curtain call eh? So then what happened?"

"The fire trucks and cops came and I was hauled off to make a statement downtown about what had happened. The crazy thing was that the cops acted like I was one who set the fire. They didn't believe someone was trying to kill me. Eventually, they let me go, but I was too scared to stay at home by myself. Can I crash here?"

"That is some rough night you had. Of course you can stay here."

"What's her name—you don't think she'll mind?"

"Who? Kelly? Nah, she isn't the jealous type. I'll get you a pillow and blanket and you can sleep out here on the couch. Tomorrow we'll see what we can do to get you inside Thorn-Corp."

"Thanks." Paige smiled. "I knew I could count on you."

Mike got up and dug an extra blanket and pillow out of the closet and handed them to Paige. She made herself a bed and was soon fast asleep.

It was early when Mike started banging around in the kitchen making espresso. Paige got up and to see what all the noise was about. She sat beside Kelly at the small table and watched as Mike made a huge mess on his counter. In spite of her near-death ordeal, she smiled at her clumsy friend, trying to impress his guests with making fancy coffee and looking like a klutz in the process.

"So where do you work," Paige asked Kelly casually as Mike set two miniature cups of messy espresso before them.

"Thorn-Corp. Well, I work for Interim, which is a temp agency, but they're sending me to Thorn-Corp today."

"Yeah," Mike said taking a seat. "I was thinking you could take her place."

"How convenient. Where on earth did you two meet then?"

"Reece's Bar."

Paige laughed. "When I said I needed to be a Kelly-Girl I was talking about the temp agency, not an actual girl named Kelly."

"Well, you got both, more or less," Kelly said. "I thought perhaps we could work on making you look more like me before you head off to work."

"Sure, what did you have in mind?"

"Dye your hair blonde, or maybe get a hold of a wig. Then we can put you in one of my outfits and add some make-up before you go out."

Paige glanced at her modest light brown hair and realized that she rarely wore much make-up. She wanted to look presentable when she interviewed people, but usually she was all about the no-nonsense pony tail and business suit look. Kelly apparently rolled a little differently. Oh well, whatever helped accomplish her goal, she thought. The less I look like myself the more likely I won't be recognized. She shrugged and acquiesced.

"Whatever. I guess."

Kelly smiled, got up, and announced that she would get her make-up kit from the car.

CHAPTER 7

Paige arrived at Thorn-Corp at eight a.m. as Kelly had instructed her to. They would need to see her driver's license at security in order to create a temporary security badge. Kelly had given Paige her driver's license for just that purpose, which is part of the reason she was disguised. The log books said that a Kelly Kalowinski was arriving and it wouldn't have worked for Paige Lynn to show up in her stead. That would have certainly have caused a commotion and gotten Paige sent back to the temp agency.

A man named Johnson issued her temp security badge, Paige was handed over to an administrative assistant named Tracy who led Paige through the maze of hallways and asked her questions about her previous experience. Luckily, Kelly had given her a copy of her resume to memorize before she started and Paige was able to rattle off a list of different companies and the duties she had performed.

Tracy showed Paige to the file room and explained the process to her. Workers from the main office would bring down invoices to the file room and stack them neatly in her box. It was up to her to file the invoices as quickly and proficiently as possible. They were already back-logged by several weeks since the last girl quit suddenly. An older lady by the name of Ruth Leonard was in charge of the file office, but she was ill and not able to keep up. Ruth would be in shortly to help her out and answer whatever other questions she might have.

There was a photocopier in the back of the room, but apparently it wasn't used often. The front desk in the office did have a computer with limited access to current files and data bases, but Ruth didn't have any need for it. The computer sat silently, waiting for someone to turn it on.

Tracy stayed with Paige for about an hour to make sure she understood what she was supposed to do. Paige grew increasingly frustrated because she was sure the most uneducated of people could file invoices. It merely required knowledge of the alphabet and an ability to count. Still, Ruth explained to Paige that some temps still struggled with it, which is why Tracy kept a watchful eye on her. Around nine in the morning Ruth rolled in and was introduced to Paige. Ruth sat and turned on the radio before she began working on one of the many boxes of files sitting in the corner. She spoke very little to Paige and then disappeared for a while for lunch.

At long last, Paige was able to search the file room for particular files she thought might help her indict Jack Noland. She first had to locate the accounting files, which had been under M&M Accounting. Maurice Metroff was listed as owner of M&M. She photocopied what she could, stuffing sheets into her oversized purse before anyone could see her. Ruth returned and she got little accomplished the rest of the afternoon. When Ruth left at three, Paige was able to find more files listing Rose St. James as an assistant who signed off on a number of questionable deals. Paige stumbled across a goldmine by accident when she was doing her assigned filing. It was four and nearly time to clock out when Paige found a purchasing invoice for a racing dog from Bob Sherman. Sherman was paid a large sum of cash and it was later written off of as tax expense of some sort. When she hunted for more on Bob Sherman, she came across a number of other purchasing invoices for time shares in the Bahamas. Paige photocopied those pages and wondered how she was going to walk out of work that day without looking like she'd stolen a ream of paper and stuck it in her purse.

Tracy reappeared as Paige was turning off the radio and the computer for Ruth and getting ready to leave. Tracy gave her a suspicious look, but did not accuse her of anything. Instead, she said, "Jack Noland has requested a meeting with you before you leave today."

"Isn't he the big wig around here?"

"Yep."

"Why would he want to waste his time talking to a temp?"

She shrugged. "I don't know, but he specifically asked me to come and get the temp named Kelly Kalowinski who started work in the file office today."

"Okay," Paige said, convinced her cover had been somehow blown. She glanced around the room, wondering if there had been surveillance cameras she hadn't noticed.

Tracy led her through the factory and into an elevator. They rode in silence to the third floor and to Jack Noland's office. Tracy strolled past a series of desks in the large open room to the back of the office. There, nestled in the corner, was Noland's private suite. Tracy knocked lightly and he called, "Come in." She swung the door open and invited Paige to enter. Once Paige had stepped inside the clean, sleek looking office, Tracy shut the door behind her and left Jack and Paige alone together.

"Come in, come in," Jack invited. He didn't look all that imposing at just under six feet tall. His blonde hair was neatly trimmed and he wore a sharp black suit. The thing that stood out the most to Paige was his piercing blue-gray eyes. They were as cold, despite the smile on his lips.

"You wanted to see me?" she said, not sure what else to say.

"Yes, I wanted take the time to greet our newest employee to Thorn-Corp."

"I'm just a temp, there's no need," she said.

"All my employees are important to me," he said as he approached her. "Particularly the pretty ones."

"Sir, I don't see what my looks have to do with my job performance. I file invoices is all."

"But you aren't just filing are you?" he said quizzically.

"I have no idea what you mean." Jack was standing uncomfortably close to her now and looking down her low cut shirt. Was he trying to unnerve her? she thought.

"Oh, I think you do *Kelly*."

"I'm sorry," she said stepping back. "I really don't know what you mean."

"The files in your purse, Paige. Surely you didn't think it would go unnoticed?"

"Paige?" She swallowed, nervous as hell, now. "I think you've mistaken me for someone else."

"Oh, no. I think you were the one who was mistaken in thinking that you could put one over on me."

"I … I, ah, I d-don't know what to say."

"Say Uncle," he said stepping back toward her again and placing his hand on her arm. He grabbed her firmly, hinting that all he had to do was twist it a bit to hurt her.

"Uncle?" she echoed, confused.

He leaned down and nearly hissed in her ear, "You see this is a game you can't win. Your friend Mike is currently in the hospital and you will soon join him if you don't give up this foolish crusade. Do you understand?"

"What happened to Mike?"

"Some thugs beat him up. That's all. Broke a couple ribs I understand. Must be quite painful, especially knowing that you are the one who's to blame for it."

"You bastard!" Paige cried, struggling to break free.

"I've been called worse and I've done worse. Do not cross me again. Empty out your purse and go home and don't ever come back here."

Paige slid her purse off of her arm and opened it up. She dumped out all the papers she'd hid and let them flutter to the floor in a mess. She stepped over the pile of papers and walked to the door.

She opened it, paused, turned around and spit out, "You may have won the battle, *but you have not won the war."* And she left, slamming the door behind her.

CHAPTER 8

Paige rushed to her car and drove straight to Clover Memorial Hospital. At the front desk she demanded to know if a Mike Mullens had been admitted. They pointed her to room 203 and she thanked them before rushing down the hallway.

She saw Mike laying in the bed, his ribs wrapped and his face looking all swollen and bruised. He was on an IV drip of painkillers. Paige walked in, nearly in tears. "I'm so sorry Mike," she said as she stepped up toward the bed.

"For what?" he said, looking at her through his one good eye.

"Jack Noland said he sent some thugs after you because of your involvement with me and the story. It's all my fault. I am really so..." she sighed, looking down, rubbing her head, then looked back down at him, "...if I thought he would do something like this, I would never have gone undercover today."

"I'm guessing your cover was blown."

"Yeah, I had a purse full of copied files to bring with me, but at the last moment Jack called me to his office and called me out."

Mike winced in pain for a second and then said, "That's too bad."

"So what happened with you?"

"I dropped Kelly off at her home and stopped to get some gas at the Marathon station downtown. A couple guys jumped out of a van and beat the crap out of me. At first I had no idea why they jumped me or who they were. I thought it was pretty random, you know, until after the ambulance brought me here. Once I got some rest and got some good drugs in me, it dawned on me that it probably wasn't really random at all."

"Maybe we should just drop this whole Noland thing."

"No, no," Mike grimaced, trying to sit up more, "Not now. Turns out they finall found Bob's body,."

"Let me guess, it was dumped in Pottersville and was labeled a John Doe?"

"You got it." Mike smiled.

"So there is nothing linking his body to Jack, except my testimony right now. I am not sure even with a body that anyone will believe me."

"There has to be more evidence linking Bob to Jack. I mean, he was on his *payroll*."

"I found some files that could be damaging, but I had to give them up before I left."

"Scott swung by and said some guy from the lab, Steve, was trying to get a hold of you as well."

"*The scarf*. I'd nearly forgotten all about it. I wonder if that will be of any help."

"What scarf?"

"Bob, or Jack, one of them, left a red scarf lying on the sidewalk. I picked it up and stuffed it in my pocket before I took off from the scene Monday. I had Steve analyze it to see if we could get any hits off it."

"Like DNA or something?"

"Yeah, something linking everything together."

"Sounds like you should go visit Steve."

"I wish I could've been there this morning. I shouldn't have tried to trick Jack like that. Why did I ever think it would work?"

"It was a good plan," Mike said reaching out to take her hand. He was silent for a moment before he added, "Besides, if you'd been with me this morning, or if you'd been at home in bed, it wouldn't have mattered. Jack knew I was working with you and he would have still come after me. The good thing is his thugs didn't beat you up, too. Now you have a chance to keep digging away at this."

She frowned, "I should have never started this."

"Someone has to take down the corporate criminals of this world. Someone has to be looking out for the little guy."

"Didn't know you were such an idealist."

"Maybe it was the blow to the head." He laughed, then grabbed at his head. "Oh, ouch. That hurts. Don't make me laugh."

Paige leaned over and kissed Mike on the forehead. "I'll be back later."

"I'll still be here," he called after her as she left the room.

Paige first paid a visit to the lab in Pottersfield. Steve was working the late shift, so she was able to catch him before he went home that night.

"What you got for me Steve," she asked as the woman let her into the lab.

Steve stepped away from the table and went over to the far corner. He picked a plastic evidence bag with the red scarf in it off the shelf and returned to Paige. "I was able to pull a couple of things from the scarf for you."

"Thanks. What did you find?"

"The blood splatters do indeed belong to the John Doe that rolled in here yesterday. They identified him as Robert John Sherman. Male, aged fifty-five. Five foot eight inches and one hundred forty-five pounds. Address is listed as three one two four five Rock Road, which is between Clover and Pottersville."

"Where was he found, exactly?"

"Sherman kept to himself, mostly, so no one ever made a missing person's report. Some workers over at the M&M Iron Mill found him in a pile of scrap iron. They didn't know who he was and the body was pretty mangled by that time. There was no wallet or ID on him, but eventually the coroner was able to use dental records to figure it out. Of course your ramblings might have been enough to point him in the right direction. I don't know. But it's now being ruled murder at least."

"That isn't good for poor Bob, but at least it's a step in the right direction toward taking down Jack Noland."

"How Bob was found wasn't the most interesting piece of information that I found, though."

"Then what is?"

"This scarf is an expensive Hermes scarf that was purchased in New York City for a Nicole Noland—at least I assume it was. The credit card in use belonged to Jack Noland, but it was Bob Sherman's signature on it. The scarf was purchased just days before Nicole's birthday and it is a woman's scarf, so it would make sense it was a gift for her."

"Why would Bob have the scarf on him the night he was murdered?"

"Maybe he was having an affair with Nicole, or maybe Nicole had discovered what kind of dirty deals Bob was really up to. Who knows?"

"This scarf connects Jack to Bob on that particular night, but I'm afraid it wouldn't be admissible in court because I took it from the crime scene myself."

"That could be a problem."

Paige took the bag from Steve and said, "Thanks."

"No problem."

Paige drove the twenty minutes back to her apartment. When she entered it was just as she had left it. There was no one waiting there to beat her up and it hadn't been trashed a second time. She let out a long sigh of relief and closed the door. She locked the deadbolt and went directly to the fridge to fix something to eat. As she pulled out the necessary accoutrements to make a peanut butter and jelly sandwich, she thought about her family that was still in Cleveland and Detroit. She was thankful they were far enough away that Jack Noland hadn't targeted them—yet anyway.

After her dinner, Paige took a long, hot shower and then crawled into bed and soon went into a sound sleep.

CHAPTER 9

Friday, March 20, 1992

Paige awoke to a loud banging on her door. Wondering who the hell would be so noisy or demanding, she glanced over at the clock; eight a.m. What day was it again? Oh yes, Friday, she remembered. Not that it mattered since was she unemployed, anyway. The incessant knocking didn't stop, so Paige threw off her covers, pulled on her bathrobe and went to answer the door.

Standing on her porch was a police officer who did not look pleased. "Can I help you?" she said politely, after reading the badge he held out, and added, "Officer Cross."

"Ms. Lynn, we would like to question you about the disappearance of Brooke Young."

"Brooke worked at the paper. She covered most of the Elementary School news and some of the High School news. What happened to her?"

"That's what we'd like to know."

Paige sighed. "Come in and give me a minute to get dressed and I'll go back to the station with you."

Cross nodded and stepped inside. Paige shut the door and then disappeared back into her bedroom to change. She threw on a pair of jeans and a t-shirt before returning to the officer. The blond wig she'd worn on Thursday was gone.

"Ready," she said lifting her purse off the dining table. Looks like Friday isn't going to be any more peaceful than the rest of the week, she thought as she followed the cop out to his car. She decided it was best to take her car, said so to Officer Cross, who nodded permission, and she turned to go back to her vehicle to follow him.

At the station, she sat in the meeting room and waited for the cops to question her. Paige wondered why they were targeting her for these disappearances and not Noland. If they were working for Noland, perhaps he'd asked them to harass her. It dawned on her that perhaps Noland had taken the time to set her up and make her the fall gal.

Maybe he had wanted Maurice to contact her and maybe he had wanted her to write that damaging op-ed type of article on him. Could it be? That seemed like a lot of work.

Officer Cross came in with a file folder and threw it down on the table. "What do you know about Brooke Young?"

"Brooke was a friend of mine from The Daily Clover. We worked together the past two and half years. She grew up in Clover and was in the band and choir in high school. She loved her high school days, which is why she decided to cover that portion of the news. She was well liked. I don't know why anyone would wish her harm."

"Maybe you were jealous of her?"

"No, I wasn't."

"Maybe she and Maurice were having an affair, so you killed him first in the fire and then came back to exact your revenge on her later!"

Paige couldn't help but laugh. The idea was so ludicrous.

"Murder is no laughing matter."

"I know," she said trying to be serious. "It's just that you're grasping at straws here. What you suggested is just ridiculous."

"Then why don't you tell me what really happened."

"Maurice Metroff was on Jack Noland's payroll until recently and he was my source for the article I wrote earlier this week. The same people who kidnapped me killed him. As for Brooke," she shrugged,

"I have no idea."

"Was Brooke on Jack's payroll, too? Maybe she was a corrupt journalist." Cross snickered as if Paige's story was somehow crazier than his own suggestions.

"Maybe she was. I don't know. I had no idea she was missing until this morning. How long has she been gone?"

"Her husband reported her missing last night when she never came home from work."

"Maybe she had an accident, or got lost, or simply left her husband. It hasn't been that long. She'll probably show up soon and this will have all been for nothing. What makes you think I had something to do with it?"

"You always seem to around when people turn up missing or dead."

"So I'm a usual suspect, huh?" Paige sighed.

"Yep."

"Why don't you let me go and do some of my own digging? If I ask around at the paper maybe I can get some answers for you."

"Maybe you're just going to take the time to cover your own tracks."

Paige shook her head and rolled her eyes. This guy had read one too many pulp fiction detective novels in his time. She decided his tough act was clearly just that—an act. "Look, Mike Mullens was attacked and I was nowhere near him at the time. Do you think I had something to do with that as well? He told me two of Jack Noland's thugs jumped out of a van and started hitting him. Perhaps you should stop wasting your time with me and start looking for those two thugs. That sounds like a good starting place don't you think?"

Officer Cross appeared taken aback by the speech. Paige had made a point, and he knew it. She could read his mind as he considered the facts of the situation—they have nothing on me to warrant them being able to hold me.

Cross shrugged and said, "You're free to leave, but stay in town in case something comes up."

"Thank you," she said taking her purse and getting up to leave. She opened the door and let herself out. Feeling drained, Paige walked the short distance to her car. She drove the block and half or so to the newspaper office and turned down the one-way street and into the parking lot behind the building.

Paige entered through the back and made her way up the old rickety stair way to Scott's office. When she knocked on his door he looked up, and looked shocked. "What are you doing here? I thought I fired you a couple days ago."

"You did," Paige said, maintaining her composure, "but a lot has gone down and I thought we should have a conversation about it at least. I'm sure we can be of help to each other right now."

"Come in and close the door."

Paige closed the door and sat in the seat across from Scott. He looked tired and stressed, but then again he always looked that way. Running a newspaper was not an easy job and it demanded a lot of sacrifices, including time away from family and friends. Paige didn't' envy him his tough position, but lately she felt like he was failing the community of Clover.

"So what exactly has gone down since your piece ran?"

"Well, for starters, I tracked down my source, only to have him murdered by Noland's thugs a few hours later. I was abducted and tossed into an old warehouse, which was then set on fire. I barely escaped with my life, but the cops wanted to play it as if I were the one to blame and they have been harassing me ever since."

"You just can't catch a break this week can you?"

"No, I can't. I went undercover at Noland's Thorn-Corp, only to be discovered at the last minute. Even though I had to hand back over the files I had access to, I was able to at least see that there is merit to Maurice Metroff's story. Jack Noland is up to no good and he is making damn sure no one else knows about it. That's why he went after Mike and Brooke Young yesterday. Mike wound up in the hospital with broken ribs and Brooke is probably dead."

"Brooke Young is dead?" Scott said in shock.

"Well, missing. The cops hauled me in for questioning about her disappearance this morning. I guess since we both worked for The Daily Clover they assumed I would know something. Perhaps they missed the memo that you fired me. I don't know."

"What does Brooke have to do with Jack Noland?"

"Nothing that I know of, but if she's the latest to disappear, we have to take into account she might have seen or heard something."

"Thanks for coming to me about this," Scott said, warming some to her. "This is definitely getting serious and something needs to be done. Why don't you go home, get some more rest and then meet me back here later tonight. Maybe by then I'll have some more info for you."

"Yeah, I could do that. What time?"

"I'll be here until seven or eight at least. Sometime around then. We can talk privately then and get this all sorted out."

"I'm thinking it's time we called in the FBI. I'm in way over my head here."

"Let me see what I can find out first and then we'll see about putting in the call together later. Deal?"

"Sure." They shook hands and she turned to leave Scott's office. As she trekked back to her car, she couldn't help but shake the feeling something was off with Scott. He was usually much less diplomatic and much more in-your-face. What happened to him to spook him so much? Had Noland gotten to him, too? Was there no one she could trust?

Back at her car, Paige decided it was time to pay Mrs. Nicole Noland a visit. She was going to confront her with the scarf and see if she couldn't get some answers. At this point, the picture of what Jack was up to was still fuzzy.

Jack and Nicole lived in a new neighborhood on the outskirts of Clover. Their house was at the end of a long lane through a small grove of trees. It was a secluded house, perfect for someone who needed to escape or go into hiding. Paige parked in front of the sprawling house, rang the door bell, and hoped Nicole would be at home.

A buxom blonde answered the door. "Can I help you?"

"Yeah, are you Nicole Noland?"

"Yes, who wants to know?"

"My name is Paige Lynn and I'm from the Daily Clover. I have a few questions I'd like to ask you."

"What about?"

"Your husband and this scarf," Paige said holding up the plastic bag with the scarf inside.

"Come in."

Paige followed Nicole down into the sunken living room and was invited to sit on a huge wrap-around sofa. Nicole sat across from her and gestured for Paige to ask away.

"Why did Bob Sherman have your scarf the day he was murdered?"

"Beats me," Nicole shrugged.

"Did you know that he had purchased the scarf as favor to your husband?"

"Yes, Jack gave me the scarf and said he'd sent someone to New York to purchase it for me. He made a big deal out of it being delivered in person."

"Are you aware that Bob Sherman's blood is on the scarf and that it implicates your husband in his murder?"

"No, I wasn't aware of the location of the scarf. It came up missing last week."

"Do you think Bob might have stolen it because Jack didn't pay him for his services?"

"It's possible I suppose. This house is monitored by a security company. I wouldn't know how Bob got a hold of it, but he may have had his ways."

"Do you think your husband is capable of murder Misses Noland?"

"He's a very shrewd businessman and can often be cold and calculating, I'll admit. Even still, I'm not sure he'd be stupid enough to go around killing people in such a small town. Of course people are going to notice."

"Well, I witnessed your husband shoot Bob Sherman in the chest. When Jack left the scene of the crime, I picked up this scarf and had it tested. Blood splatters on it link it to Bob, who has recently been identified as the John Doe that was found at the Iron Mills dump site. And, purchasing invoices link the scarf to you Nicole."

Nicole didn't appear to be terribly upset, merely annoyed. She blew out a long breath and eventually said, "I think it's time for my husband to get a lawyer. This has gone too far."

"I'd say it has. His thugs killed Maurice Metroff, beat up Mike Mullens and now, I have a feeling, they're involved in the disappearance of one Brooke Young. Did you know Misses Young?"

"Brooke Young was a friend of mine. Our sons are in the same grade at Clover Leaf Elementary. She was a good woman. I don't know why anybody would want to do her harm. I'm sorry to hear she's missing. Any leads?"

"None, but the police did haul me in for questioning. Brooke and I both worked for The Daily Clover and I guess they thought that was connection enough."

"Well, thank you for dropping by to let me know what's been going on. I appreciate it." Nicole stood, indicating it was time for Paige to leave. "Now, if you will excuse me, I have some business to attend to."

"Sure," Paige said, also rising to her feet. Although she didn't say anything more, she got the distinct feeling Nicole knew much more. Even if she didn't have a hand in her husband's affairs, she wasn't exactly blind to them. If the FBI investigated, would that mean that Nicole would have charges pressed against her as well?

Still going over the conversation in her head, Paige got in her car. She noticed Nicole watching her through a window as she pulled out of the drive. Perhaps she had made a mistake in showing up at the Noland's house. What if she alerted Jack and they both fled Clover forever? She supposed it was better than continuing the killing spree, but if they fled, justice would never be served would it.

CHAPTER 10

Paige drove out to Clover Memorial Hospital to visit Mike once again and to let him know what had happened. He was resting as comfortable as possible with three broken ribs. She sat beside him and explained everything.

"So the police woke me up this morning to take me in for questioning. Seems as if Brooke Young has come up missing as well, and they thought I might have something to do with it."

"That's ridiculous."

"I know. It's starting to look more and more like the police are on Noland's payroll and he's having them harass me."

"So what did you do?"

"I told them to look for the thugs that beat you up and left. They really didn't have any evidence to hold me, so I knew I was free to go."

"Awesome," he said and smiled.

"Then I spoke to Scott and he was acting suspicious."

"What do you mean?"

"I told him about all the evidence mounting against Noland and he wanted to discuss it later, when nobody was around. He acted ... I don't know ... paranoid."

"It could be a trap. Scott may very well be in on this, too. It wouldn't surprise me."

"You really don't think Scott would sell out to some corporate creep like Jack Noland do you? That goes against the whole checks and balances of the system. We're supposed to be the eyes and ears for the people and stand up against corruption."

"Yeah, but it's a small time paper that could be on the verge of shutting down at any moment. Maybe he did what he thought he had to in order to keep the paper running. I don't know."

"But murder? Isn't that more than a little extreme to keep things running the way they are?"

"To the average person, but Noland isn't playing with a full deck. Maybe Scott isn't either."

"I spoke to Noland's wife, Nicole, this afternoon, too."

"And?"

"She didn't seem too surprised at the accusations I made against Jack, but I don't know if she's his accomplice or not. I can't help but feel she was getting ready to run."

"They may very well run. Have you contacted the FBI yet?"

"No, Scott said we should wait."

"Well, then I say definitely call them. Call them from here before you leave the hospital."

"When are you getting out of here?"

"Tomorrow, actually."

"Who's picking you up?"

"My sister."

"Good."

They chatted some more about family and other odds and ends before Paige gave him a kiss on the forehead and left. She swung by the nurses' station to use the phone. From there she used the phone book to look up the local FBI office. She called them and got an automated service which instructed her to leave a detailed message. With a long sigh, Paige gave them her name, address, phone number and brief summary of why she was calling. Before she hung up, she was informed it may take several days to several weeks before someone returned her call. Paige prayed it wasn't too late by the time they got back to her.

Overstressed, Paige went to Reece's for her nightly beer and burger. It felt odd to be there without Mike by her side. She had come to rely on his company over the past year they'd worked together. They'd become best buds in a lot of ways, but she'd never thought of him in romantic terms. Now that he was lying in a hospital bed because of her, she had started to realize that there was more there than she first thought. Paige ordered a second beer after her burger was finished. One was usually her limit, but two felt necessary after the past week from hell.

She checked her watch to see that it was only seven p.m. Scott wanted to meet at eight. Perhaps she should show up a little early, maybe throw him off some. Not to mention the fact that she was exhausted and just wanted to go home and crawl into bed. The last thing she needed was a late night meeting that may or may not be a deadly trap. Reluctantly, Paige paid her bill and left for the newspaper office.

When Paige arrived through the back door, there was no one around, which was unusual. She wondered, where were the maintenance men who constantly guarded the printers? For that matter, where were the printers who worked day and night? And there was always a reporter or two hanging out in the office, struggling to meet a deadline. Had everyone gone home for the night?

She made her way up the old steps to Scott's office, but Scott was not there. Odd, she thought. The light was on and his computer was still whirring away in the corner. He had to be around there somewhere.

"Scott?" she called.

No one answered.

"Scott?"

Paige turned and walked out into the news office. The overhead lights were on, but no one was at any of the desks. Paige heard footsteps overhead. She looked up at the old ceiling, complete with ancient pipes and duct work from the turn of the century. Sometimes it rattled and made weird noises on its own, but she was fairly certain that the noise she heard wasn't normal. It sounded as if it were coming from the third floor. No one was ever on the third floor.

At one time the third floor housed the newspaper office, but eventually it became too costly to run such a large office. Budget cuts over the years had reduced the staff to the crowded office space in front of the printers. Now the third floor was an unofficial archive and place for spare printer parts. No one ventured up there because it was a gigantic mess.

There was a long silence, and then more footsteps. Paige drew in a deep breath and prepared herself for the daunting task of visiting the third floor. She stepped out of the newspaper office and found the stairway that led up to the old office area. A single naked light bulb lit her way up the dark and narrow stairwell. The stairs creaked eerily beneath her weight. What would she find up there?

"Scott?" she called when she reached the top of the stairs. "Is that you up here?"

Paige flipped the switch and the neon lights flickered on above her. The light in the far corner was only on a moment before burning out, but at least the light closest to her remained on. She stepped onto the wooden floor and looked around the piles of papers and filing cabinets. Slowly, and cautiously, she explored the maze of printer parts and old office furniture.

She tripped over something in the middle of the floor and fell with an undignified thud. "Damn it." What had she tripped over? Paige saw it was a dark pile on the floor, something wrapped in a tarp. She pulled back the tarp just enough to reveal Brooke's cold, lifeless eyes staring back up at her. Paige screamed and jumped back.

"You shouldn't have interfered," a voice called from the shadows.

"Jack?"

Jack Noland emerged from the shadows and into the dim light filtering in from the uncovered front windows that looked out onto the Main Street below. "Yes."

Paige pulled herself into a standing position and faced Jack Noland once again. "What are you doing here?"

"I might ask you the same question, but I think we both know the answer to that."

"Why did you kill Brooke?"

"She knew too much, just as you do."

"Are you planning to kill me, too?"

"That's the plan."

"How many bodies does that make? Three? Plus a man in the hospital. This is getting to be quite messy, don't you think? Perhaps you should quit while you are ahead."

"But I'm not ahead. I still have much work to do before I control all of Clover."

"Why bother? Clover is such a boring town. Certainly there are bigger and better towns to try and take over."

"Yes, but Clover holds a special place in my heart." Jack stepped toward her.

"If you kill me, that will only make you look guiltier. I promise not to print another word about you. Hell, I won't print another word period. Scott fired me, so it isn't like I'm really a threat to you anymore."

"Just like a reporter, trying to talk her way out of her own death. Your bargaining skills won't help you here."

"Just tell me how you plan to kill me? Are you going to shoot me like you did Bob?"

"Yes, that seems like the best way," Jack said, taking his gun out of his shoulder holster.

"You get that piece from the police, Jack? The same police you're paying off to look the other way while you do your dirty deeds?"

"Officer Cross is one of the men on my payroll. People are incredibly easy to corrupt."

Run, Paige decided. She ducked behind a huge metal filing cabinet and started to crawl across the floor back toward the stairway.

Jack wasn't fooled. He knew what she was up to. Before Paige could get very far, Jack reached down and grabbed her by her shirt. He yanked her up to where he could see her. "You didn't think you could get away that easily did you?"

"Well, yeah." She smiled sheepishly. Paige started struggling, kicking against him. She managed to kick him in the shins and cause him a great deal of pain. He dropped her and she broke into a run through office.

"Come back here you bitch!"

As if by magic, the door to office slammed and locked shut. Was it Scott or one of Jack's thugs she wondered? In any case, she was now trapped up on the third floor with a homicidal maniac. How on earth was she going to get out of this one?

"You can't escape!" Jack called after her. "That is not how your story ends."

"You wanna bet," Paige growled as she started to find her away back toward the front of the office. Perhaps she could open a window and climb out the old fire escape.

Jack must have seen her moving through the rows of boxes and cabinets—he took a shot at her. The gun echoed loudly and the bullet imbedded itself in one of the steel cabinets. Paige stumbled over some printer parts and broken chairs before she made it back up to the front of the office. Jack was clamoring after her, making a racket as he knocked over stacks of papers and metal poles.

Paige reached the window and unlocked it. She pushed and pulled at it, but it wasn't budging. She wasn't sure if it had been painted over or if the wood had gotten damp and warped. Either way, the window wasn't going to open. She moved to the next window. That one whined and squeaked as she cracked it open. But she didn't have time to work it any further up, Jack was standing right in front of her again. She looked up to see the barrel of a gun staring at her.

Instinct kicked in. Paige took her purse off her shoulder and swung it at the gun. It was knocked out of Jack's hand and skidded across the floor. As he went to search for it, Paige remembered she still had Mike's gun. She dug in her purse, pulled it out, turned off the safety and pointed it at Jack.

"Shoe's on the other foot now."

He looked up, but didn't seem fazed by the fact that she was now wielding a weapon.

Jack ducked down onto the floor and felt around, looking for his gun. He grunted in disgust, jumped to his feet and ran toward her full force. He's going to try and knock me out of the window and kill me that way, Paige thought. She stepped to the side at the last second and watched as Jack went head-long through the plate glass window. It shattered and he tumbled helplessly three floors to his death on the sidewalk below.

Paige gulped and looked down through the broken window. A crowd was beginning to gather around the body. Blood seeped out around him in a big, dark pool. Sirens sounded as police came flying out of their den down the road. They blocked off the area and began their work. Paige stepped away from the window and back into the shadows.

Just like that, it was over. No more Jack Noland.

April 1992

Paige looked up from her article she was writing on the Kurdish Refugees when she noticed several co-workers standing in front of her desk.

"I'm so glad you decided to come back to the paper," Bill said.

"Me too," a smiling Mike said from his place sitting on the corner of her desk.

"We're all glad," Lynda said.

"Why didn't you take the job as editor?" Mike wanted to know.

"Too many politics involved."

"So I wonder what our new editor will be like," Bill said.

"I hear he just came back from a tour with the Peace Corps or something," Mike said. "He's real hard core."

"Yeah, I read he spent time in Mauritania, Africa," Paige added. "That's why I recommended him. His article on how everyone should own their own goat really touched me."

Mike chuckled. "And why does he think everyone should own their own goat?"

"Something about responsibility and perspective, I believe. He takes a very different approach to things than Scott did, which is what I was looking for."

"So are you happy with the way things turned out?" Mike asked Paige as Bill and Lynda returned to their respective desks.

"I'm not sure. Had I been able to, I might have written the ending of this story differently."

"What do you mean?"

"I don't know." Paige shrugged. "Jack had said my story didn't end with my escape, but I guess he was wrong. I just wish Bob, Maurice and Brooke had escaped as well."

"Well, Jack is dead, too. That has to count for something."

"I'm just thankful they ruled it an accident. I'm positive Officer Cross was just itching to charge me with manslaughter, or murder, or something."

"Maybe. Maybe you did Officer Cross a favor. He might not have liked being on Jack Noland's payroll."

Paige shrugged. "Nicole's off the hook, too. Her and her son get to go on living in Clover as if nothing had happened."

"I think this story has ended well," Mike said still smiling, "But there is one thing I think is missing."

"What?"

"This," he said, sliding off the desk and coming around to her seat. Mike leaned down and placed a kiss right on her lips. Stunned at first, Paige didn't pull away. The office broke in to a round of applause as Mike pulled away in triumph.

Out of Control

CHAPTER 1

He hoped he didn't have to use his gun. Jake Luder didn't like big complicated messes; he had gotten into one too many already. Even still, he preferred his life of crime to the alternatives: a job, or jail. They were one in the same to him. At thirty-three he had lived fast and hard. He'd robbed his first convenience store at nineteen on a dare and a coke high. From then on, he was hooked. But, he didn't do the robbery thing often. Jake mostly got his money buying and selling drugs and stolen goods. Now and again he did find a straight forward odd job for someone. He'd dabbled in factory work, retail and other boring jobs, but never lingered long at any one place. For him, robbing stores was reserved for emergency cash only.

This was an emergency. He'd sold all the drugs he could get his hands on and gambled away all of his profits. He'd trashed his car and burned a lot of bridges with his former connections. Now he was stuck in the small town of Vancouver, New York. Jake's brother and partner in crime were currently stealing the getaway car while Jake was casing the place they planned to rob: *Anderson Carryout*

The sign above the building was faded along with the old Pepsi sign above it. A newer sign with a light was unceremoniously stuck in the yard in front of the old one. Jake guessed it had been too much trouble or too expensive to bother with removing the old sign. Kids and adults came and went in a steady stream. Finally, the place appeared to be empty except for the three employees. One of the employees left. This was as easy as it would get.

Jake decided to go for it. He loaded his gun and shoved it down the front of his pants. He drew in a deep breath and pulled a ski mask on over his face. His pulse quickened as his heart beat wildly. The rush of adrenalin right before a job was always such a wonderful feeling. In that moment, Jake felt like he was all-powerful. He was God in that moment.

Inside, Jill and Téa were going about their normal business. Jill went to the back room to get stock during this slow time. Téa phoned her friend and then went to find the pricing gun.

Jake slipped inside and approached the old fashioned wooden counter. Before he could announce his presence, the door opened yet again. He turned to see a tall slim girl enter the store. She was no more than seventeen or eighteen years old and the most beautiful thing he'd ever seen. A man in his thirties came in behind her. Oh shit, Jake thought. Two more people were going to witness the robbery and that made it much more complicated. Oh well, can't back out now, he told himself. He looked more than a little suspicious in his ski mask. He needed to demand their attention before he lost control of the situation. "Give me all your money now," he yelled at the girl behind the counter.

Téa was as much surprised as she was scared. Robberies happened on TV or in the movies—not in real life. Not in tiny Vancouver, a tiny rural town where everyone knew everyone else. It had to be a prank, she thought.

"Give me all your money. Now," he yelled again.

Jill came out of the storage room. When she saw the man in the ski mask she dropped her box of Snapple. The box landed with a heavy thud and there was the sound of glass shattering.

Startled by her sudden appearance, Jake whipped out his gun and pointed it at Jill. This was going too slow, he thought. He pointed from Jill to the cash register with the gun. "Open the drawer."

Hands shaking uncontrollably, Téa opened the drawer. She reached her hands into the till and took a bunch of ones, fives, tens and twenties. Her purple nails scratched Jake accidently as she shoved the bills into his outstretched hands. Téa started to reach in again for more money as Jake snatched a plastic bag and shoved the money into that, but she stopped. Instead of pulling out more money, Téa hit the panic button underneath the counter while Jake was busy with the bag. She didn't think he noticed her pausing before grabbing the rest of the bills, but he did. Jake looked up to see Téa hitting the button and she missed the bag. Bills fluttered to the ground, but no one bothered to pick them up.

"Ah, shit. Why'd you have to go and hit the fucking button?"

The alarm was tripped and the cops were on their way. Téa wasn't sure what would happen next. Would he shoot her for sounding the alarm on him? Would it be worth dying over, she wondered.

"Bitch," he muttered. "Get over here," he yelled. He ripped off his ski mask, revealing his short and unusually bright blond hair that made his green eyes stand out substantially.

Téa found something charming about him. Realizing she should be afraid instead of studying his features, Téa jumped to attention and did exactly as he said. She came out from around the counter and stood beside him and the two unlucky customers who'd wandered in at the wrong time. Pointing the gun at them the whole time, Jake went over to the cash register and cleaned it out. Téa guessed he'd gotten eight hundred to a thousand dollars. It was a good chunk of change for the small town business owners, but not what she thought was worth going to prison over. Téa felt personally violated and knew her boss would be crushed by the robbery.

Jake finished taking the money and looked up to say, "Is there a back way out of this place?"

Jill pointed to the storage room and managed to say, "Back there," Jill felt as if she were watching a movie.

Jake, still waving the gun around, ordered all of them to get in the back room. At that moment, the police pulled up. Normally cool, Jake was on edge and near panic. "Go out there and tell them I have hostages and I will shoot them if they try to fuck with me." Jake turned to the rest and said, "Now you guys get in the back room"

Jill, relieved to be safe, dashed out the door toward the flashing lights. A light rain had begun to fall. Four policemen surrounded her as soon as she emerged. They comforted and questioned her. Jill gave them the description of the robber, told them what happened and delivered the message he'd given her. The police decided to call in a negotiator.

Meanwhile, Téa and the two customers walked into the back storage room. Jake pushed the boxes and junk from in front of the back door. "This is a fire hazard you know," he said, as he was finally able to open the door enough to get out. Jake looked around. He could see the flashing lights coming from cop cars out front, illuminating an alley around the corner. He heard the rumble of an old car and decided to pull Téa and the two customers out into the ally with him. A truck came speeding down the alley and screeched to a halt.

"Thank God," Jake cried when the truck stopped. He knew it was buddy Paul. "Where the hell've you been?"

Paul tossed his cigarette out into the ally. "Genius takes time. What the hell were you doing? Throwing a party?"

"These are hostages. Get them in the truck."

Paul threw open the passenger door. Joely climbed in first followed by Fox and Téa. It was a big truck, but Téa still had to sit half on Jake's lap and half on Fox's lap. Jake slammed shut the rusty red and gray door and squished them in tightly. "Cops are dead ahead," Jake told Paul once they were all sandwiched inside.

"Then we go dead backward," Paul said and laughed. He threw the truck in reverse and sped backwards down the alley and out onto the street behind the carryout. They raced forward along the side street to the main road. There, they passed cars, crossing the double yellow lines and weaved their way through the narrow streets of Vancouver. No cops saw them escape and, despite their erratic driving, no cops followed them. Within minutes of their escape, they were on a highway, going a legal 75 miles an hour.

Jake let out a huge sigh after they made it safely out of the town. "Thought I was fucked for sure. That was the easiest fucking get away ever I saw. Those cops are complete idiots."

"Cool," is all Paul said.

"What are you going to do with us," Téa asked.

"I haven't decided yet," Jake said, "But I think it's time to get to know one another. After all, we are going to be spending a lot of time together. I'll go first. My name is Jake and I'll be your robber and captor today. See? How easy was that?"

"I'm Téa."

"Fox," the man said.

"Joely," the other woman said.

"Paul," taking another cigarette from his front shirt pocket and lighting it. He inhaled deeply.

"Can I have one," Joely asked.

"Sure," Paul said, handing her a cigarette and his lighter.

"Now that we know each other we can rely on one another like team. I get caught, you get killed. If you want to stay alive you help us make a clean get away. Understand?"

Joely inhaled and blew smoke up toward the roof of the cab. "Why do you need us? You already made your clean get away."

Fox, who'd been silent up to this point said, "Because we can identify him."

"That was real smart taking off your mask," Joely said. She seemed to have no fear where these thugs were concerned. Téa wondered if Joely was really such a bad ass or if it was all an act.

"I hate wearing that thing. It's so hot and itchy. Besides, this is much more fun." Jake smiled.

CHAPTER 2

Téa shook her head. Unbelievable. One moment my life is dull and boring with college classes and a crappy part time job and the next my life is totally changed forever. Everything had been turned upside down and all around and she had no idea what was going to happen next. It was crazy. "This is insane." she exclaimed.

"And isn't it wonderful?" Jake said. Then he and Paul began talking about what they were going to do and where they were heading. It was decided they would get a motel room, get some rest and then in the morning find their pal Brad's house. Brad lived in Staten Island. Joely, Téa and Fox would have to tag along until Jake could figure out how to best deal with them. He was unsure of how to keep them quiet after he let them go, so he needed more time to think. He didn't want to outright kill them, but there wasn't much else he could do other than keep them captive.

As Paul pulled into a Super 8 Motel, Jake explained to his hostages, "I'll be fun to play it by ear and see what happens. This could be the biggest adventure of your lives."

Paul parked and ran inside to get a couple of rooms for them.

"You'd think," Joely said, "With all the money you stole you could afford a better place for us to all stay."

"True, but that isn't what one would expect is it," Jake answered.

"And you couldn't do what was expected of you. Could you?" Fox said.

Jake smiled. "Nope."

When Paul came back in with two motel room keys he explained, "One for us and one for them."

Jake scowled. "No. It should have been one for all of us so we can keep an eye on them."

"Oh well, they are adjoining rooms. We can figure out the sleeping arrangements later."

"I suppose." Jake sighed. "We'll just have to keep the door open between the two. Let's go and get settled in already."

They drove around and parked by doors 8 and 9. They entered room 9 and Jake opened up the connecting door. Jake had Paul run out and switched license plates with another car and then make a run for food. Jake kept Joely, Fox and Téa on the two beds in the one room. Téa sat on the first bed and looked around at the green bed spread and then up at the yellowed walls—no doubt stained from cigarette smoke and age. A fairly decent TV sat on the wooden dresser against the wall. There were three boring paintings hanging on the walls and then she noticed the bathroom and guessed it was lacking a window to escape.

Fox also looked around. "Lovely."

"Hey, it'll do," Jake said defensively. He went to the desk in the corner and emptied out the bag he'd filled with money earlier. He counted the money to see how much they'd manage to snatch.

Fox sat on the edge of the bed next to Téa. Joely had taken the second bed all to herself and was restless. "I hope Paul comes back with the food soon. I'm starving. I was starving in the first place, which is why I walked into Anderson's."

Jake ignored her, but Fox responded. "I just wanted coffee and a newspaper."

"How heartbreaking," Joely said.

"Well," Fox said, "it is. None of us went in there tonight with the plan of getting kidnapped. And I'm sure none of our families counted on it, either."

Téa's eyes shot wide and she gasped. "Mom is going to be devastated."

Joely shrugged. "Well, I really don't have any family."

"I do, but I haven't seen them in forever," Fox added.

"Ah, poor baby," Joely teased.

Téa rolled her eyes. "Do you have to be so negative and sarcastic all the time?"

"Yes."

Jake huffed and slammed his fist against the wall. "Shut up! I can't hear myself think with all this fucking babbling!"

"Excuse me," Joely said, "but what else are we supposed to do?"

"Fine, talk then. Just do it quietly."

Joely leaned in closer to Téa and Fox. "I guess he's not used to having hostages any more than we are being hostages."

"Appears so," Fox said.

Téa raised an open palm in the air. "So what do we do?"

Fox motioned for them to keep it down and spoke low. "I'd say go along with him until we see a chance," Fox said. He stopped and glanced over at Jake to see if he was listening.

"Sounds good," Joely said.

"How can you two be so calm," Téa asked, "We're hostages for Chrissake."

"Easy," Joely said, "He didn't kill us and he hasn't done anything really cruel or violent. The fact that he has a gun keeps us from walking away, but it doesn't mean we don't have some control."

"Besides," Fox said, "no use in worrying over what may or may not happen. We need to just go with the flow for now. Panicking won't do us any good."

"Sounds like good advice," Jake said. He had put the money in a bright orange fanny pack, which looked absolutely ridiculous, but then it was an unlikely thing to do, which Jake prided himself on. "Like the chick said, I'm not going to hurt you if I don't have to. I'd like to keep this hostage situation as stress-free as possible."

"You're nothing like I expected," Téa said.

"What—like an asshole?"

"Well, yeah."

"I assure you, I can be an asshole at times, but I prefer to be a fun loving criminal whenever possible."

"Fun loving criminal." Joely laughed. "Like the band?"

"They stole it from me. Too bad I didn't get the rights to the name or I wouldn't have to rob people to earn a living."

Paul came back with McDonald's food for all. He handed Jake his chicken nuggets and said, "I also got a Big Mac, a fish, a double cheeseburger and a plain hamburger. You can decide who gets what." He set down three bags. Joely seized the Big Mac, Fox the double cheese and Téa the fish. They ate eagerly and quickly.

Joely commented half way through her sandwich, "This is good, but Jesus you guys act like you are on a budget or something."

Paul looked at her with deadpan irony. "What would you prefer? Sushi?"

"No, but maybe some steak or chicken parmesan would be good. Or Lobster. Lobster sounds really good."

Jake shook his head. "You're such a skinny thing. Hard to believe you could eat so much."

"Only rich people eat lobster," Paul said, "You must be a rich bitch."

"I am *not rich,* but I can be a bitch at times. Yes."

They finished eating and talked a bit more. Jake sat in a chair by the door and Paul ended up closing the door to the adjoining room and slept on the floor next to it. Jake and Paul slept soundly despite not looking at ease. Their captors didn't sleep so well.

"You awake?" Téa whispered to Fox.

Fox turned his back so he was now looking at her. Their faces were only inches apart. "No."

"Me neither. I just keep thinking about my family and wondering if I will ever see them again."

"I just wonder if life will ever be the same after this."

"It's scary isn't it?"

"Yes, but at least none of us are alone."

"True," Téa said turning onto her back. A moment later she turned onto her other side and wordlessly, Fox threw his arm around her and held her close. Téa smiled and snuggled closer before both of them fell asleep.

CHAPTER 3

It was eleven a.m. when Jake got up and roused everyone else. They took turns using the bathroom and then checked out. Jake stole the minivan next door while Jake dumped their vehicle by crashing it into some nearby woods. Joely sat in the van's back seat and Fox and Téa took the middle row. Jake found a 70's rocks station as they headed off to New York City.

Above the song *Free Bird* Joely yelled, "At least you guys aren't so stupid."

"What?" Jake hollered. He turned down the radio so he could hear her better.

"I said at least you guys aren't so stupid."

"And just what do you mean by that," Jake asked glancing back.

"I was just remembering some stories I'd heard about stupid criminals. There was this one guy who was so drunk he held up a library instead of the liquor store across the street." She laughed.

"Oh, I've done my share stupid things," Jake said.

"Oh yeah," Paul agreed. "Like the time you were on acid and tried to steal that door."

"A door?" Téa laughed. "Why the hell did you try to steal a door?"

"Maybe he thought the door was a person," Fox said.

"No," Jake said, "I thought it was a huge safe that someone had just left there. I thought no one was around so it would be okay to try and pick it up and carry it away." Jake explained.

"Did you get it?" Joely asked.

"I broke the door within a few minutes and our friend Brad grabbed me and pulled me away. I didn't get caught or anything—just laughed at."

"You were lucky, damn lucky," Fox said.

"Why do you say that?"

"How many times have you knocked over a convenience store?"

"Oh, about twenty times or so. Why?"

"One person can only get away with a crime so many times before they get caught. Your luck is probably running out right now."

"Maybe, maybe not," Jake said, turning the radio back up.

Téa turned to Fox and said, "You really think that?"

"Yeah."

The rest of the ride was uneventful except for the fact Paul got a little paranoid. Jake was doing 75 in a 55 and passed a cop. Paul was sure they were going to get pulled over and busted for the robbery.

"He didn't even see us," Jake said, then groaned as he glanced in the mirror.

The cop turned on his lights and turned around. Jake blew out air, flapping his lips as he watched in the rearview mirror. "I guess I was wrong. He did see us."

"We're fucked," Paul said.

"No," Jake said as he slowed down. The squad car was right behind them as Jake pulled over. The cop parked behind him and got out. Jake turned the radio off and said, "Okay everyone, play it cool. Any one of you panic and there ***will*** be bloodshed! So just chill out."

Everyone nodded and Jake rolled the window down. "License, registration and proof of insurance, please?"

"Hold on," Jake said as he dug into the glove compartment. He found the registration, but he knew it wouldn't help to show it. Praying for a miracle, he handed the cop the paperwork and then reached into his back pocket to get his wallet. He pulled out his license, fake of course, and handed that to the cop as well.

"This isn't your van, Mister Christian," the officer said from behind his reflective sunglasses.

"Nope, it's my friend's over here," Jake said pointing to Paul.

"So are you Mister Bell, sir?"

"Yep." Paul smiled, hoping the officer didn't ask for his license as well.

"So where were you going in such a hurry and why is Mister Christian driving?"

"We were coming from," Jake paused, trying to remember what the license plate said, "Ohio. We're driving from Ohio to New York City for a funeral and are running late. All the flights were booked and the quickest way for us was to drive. We're taking turns driving so we can go straight through."

"Oh," the officer said. He was about to say something when he got a call over his radio. There had been a homicide and he was needed as back up. He responded, telling the dispatch he was just a couple miles out and would be there shortly. He turned his attention back to the speeders at hand. Not wanting to waste valuable time doing paperwork, the officer said, "Well, watch your speed. And I'm sorry about the funeral." He handed back Jake's fake license and real registration. "Have a good day," he said turning back to his car.

Jake rolled up the window and put everything away. It wasn't until they were back on the highway that he yelled, "Yeah!"

Téa laughed, "Why is it I get the third degree and a ticket for every minor little offense when I get pulled over, but Jake gets a *have a good day* and sent on his way?"

"How many speeding tickets," Fox asked her.

"A few," Téa said.

CHAPTER 4

Hours later they arrived at their destination. The large, upscale house was on the edge of the island. It was sleek and modern. There were tall windows that let in an abundance of natural light and a view of the elaborate of landscaping around the property. Jake parked in front of the garage and opened his door. Once he got out, everyone else followed. Téa, Fox, and Joely thought it was nice to walk after all those hours of riding. Jake went up to the door and rang the bell.

It was only a couple minutes before the door opened. A young man with moussed Play-Doh yellow colored hair and one earring answered. His face lit up with a wide welcome smile when he saw Jake. "Hey man!

"Brad, how you doin' man?"

"Good. What's with your entourage?"

"Hostages."

"Really?" Brad looked surprised.

Jake smiled. "Well, they are more like a captive audience for our adventure."

Brad put his hand to his cheek and shook his head. "What did you do this time?"

"Got some emergency cash and hit a couple of snags. Well, three to be exact, but it's cool, though. We got a handle on it."

"Come in. Don't just stand there." Brad moved from the door and wandered down the hallway. He stepped down into the sunken living room, bumped into the sofa, and bent over a glass table where reached for a plastic bag.

Paul and Jake followed along with the hostages. Brad opened the bag and dropped a quarter sized-rock of dope on the table. He used his razor to cut a chunk of coke, then worked it into a soft powder, which he scraped and aligned into long, thin lines. He picked up twenty dollar bill, rolled it into a tight straw and snorted two of the lines. Brad handed Jake the bill and he did a line, and then passed the bill to Paul. Brad cut three more lines and those quickly disappeared.

Brad looked up, his eyes wide and dilated and said to the hostages, "You guys want some?"

They shook their heads no.

Brad turned his attention to Jake. "How much this time? How much you spending?"

"Enough."

A woman came from the kitchen and stepped down into the living room. The blonde had a glass of brown liquor in her hand. Brad grinned and waved everyone's attention her way. "This is Nora. Come here darling."

She came toward them and sat on the arm of a nearby chair. "Who are our guests?"

"Paul and Jake brought some new friends," Brad said.

Nora looked at Téa, Fox and Joely. "You guys bored?"

"Tired," Téa said.

"Hungry," Joely said.

"Well," Nora said, "Help yourself. The kitchen is over there." She pointed to where she'd come from. "The back bedroom is ours, but the other two are open if you want to rest. Bathroom is on the left down the hallway there."

"Was that the five cent tour?" Fox asked Nora.

"Nope, the two cent one. Feel free to wander around if you want." Nora shrugged and took another drink from her glass.

Joely wandered into the kitchen; Fox and Téa followed. Joely opened the fridge and pulled out a can of Mountain Dew. She handed it to Téa and got another one for Fox. Fox didn't take it, but instead reached in and pulled out a Pepsi. Téa drank her Mountain Dew while Joely rummaged through the cupboards and pantries. Finally, Joely sat at the kitchen bar with an apple and a bag of Doritos. Fox and Téa sat beside Joely her and also dug into the Doritos.

"So what do you think is going to happen," asked Fox.

"Who knows," Téa said

"Who cares? We're out of danger now. He would have killed us by now if he was going to," Joely said. "We should leave tonight."

Téa frowned. "And go where?"

"Home," Fox said.

"Anywhere," Joely said.

Téa said, "What if he comes after us?"

Joely sighed. "You have no sense of adventure. You should be more free-spirited."

"Yes, you do worry too much. You need to loosen up and be more confident," Fox said.

"I know, it's just ..." Téa looked down, scratching her head, "... this just this all seems so insane." She lifted her gaze back up to them, "I mean, this is like totally freaky. I don't get it. Why aren't you guys freaking out, too?"

"Just accept it," Joely said gulping down the last of her drink.

"All right then, what do you want to do?"

"We chill out, make ourselves at home and, at about two thirty am or three a.m., we meet some place here and then leave together."

"Vague, but good," Fox said. "Where do we meet? What door do we go out? Are we walking or stealing a vehicle? Or maybe we could catch a cab?"

Joely smiled. "A cab might not be a bad idea, but I was thinking we could just walk. We're just going to have to explore the house first before we know what exit is best to take and where's the safest place to meet up. It's not like I'm from the psychic friends network. Jeez."

Fox nodded, pursed his lips. "Okay."

Jake came into the kitchen and said, "Comfortable?" He was smiling and obviously high. He got a bottle of wine and some whipped cream and went up the back to the master bedroom. They didn't know if he planned on seducing Nora or if they were having a threesome or what, but they didn't really care.

Joely slipped off her barstool and found her way to the bathroom.

Fox turned to Téa and said, "That just leaves us."

"Yeah," Téa said, her discomfort rising. She was feeling a little scared, but not of Jake or Paul or Brad. She was fearful of how intense her feelings were for Fox. She had had plenty of boyfriends before and had sex with a number of them, but she wasn't one to fall so quickly. She'd already slept in the same bed as Fox and found herself wanting to do more than just sleep with him.

"Let's explore a little,' Fox said as they headed toward the hallway. Fox turned around, peered into the dining room and continued back through the kitchen. Téa followed silently. Fox looked all around taking careful note of the layout of the place. Téa peered through a window, longing for freedom, and then realized she had to speed up to catch up to Fox, who was going through yet another doorway. Téa wished she lived in such a swanky place. Fox noticed a door leading into the basement.

Fox and Téa descended the stairs. The floor was carpeted and the basement finished. There was a pool table, dart board, TV and bar in the room along with a fine leather couch. The other side of basement was dark, but it didn't matter, it appeared to hold only boxes of stored items.

At the end of the room Fox spotted a door to the outside. He made his way over and tried the door. It opened out into the wooded backyard. "Bingo!" he said.

"Our way out," Téa said.

They made their way back upstairs and down the hall. They passed by the master bedroom and heard loud noises coming from inside. Téa and Fox looked at each other and smiled, then continued on. They found an empty room they could sleep in. Joely was already lying down.

Fox sat on the bed and said in a hushed voice, "Okay, we know our way out is through the basement. We should talk to Joely about it and set up a time to meet down there."

"Hopefully we'll have at least an hour head start before anyone discovers we're missing," Téa said.

"I'm guessing they won't even bother to come after us once they notice we're gone. I'd say we get more like a four or five hour head start. They aren't going to come check on us with them being all high and everything."

"It will be a relief to get home."

"Yes, but things will be different."

"I suppose they will." Téa sighed.

"Don't worry about it," Fox said lying down. "We should try to get some sleep before we leave."

Téa lay beside him and was silent for a few moments. "Where will you go," she suddenly asked. "I mean, where do you live?"

"I live in Sawyer, Mississippi."

"Really? What were you doing in Vancouver, then?"

"I was on my way to visit relatives."

"I thought you weren't close to them."

"I'm not. I was going to make a surprise stop. I was running away, sorta, and was going to stay there."

Téa propped herself up on one hand. "Running from what?" She looked down into his brown eyes.

"A boring life."

"Guess you found what you were looking for?" She smiled.

"Not exactly what I had in mind. I was a research assistant to my college professor. We were researching deviant behavior. It was a large category and there were aspects we studied that had changed so much over the years. I thought perhaps I'd do better being an FBI agent or detective, or maybe a writer of pulp fiction. I don't know. The world of academia just wasn't for me and I didn't know what other job to get that didn't involve retail or food service."

"I thought you were some big business man when you came in."

"I'd dressed up in the hopes of applying for some jobs along the way. I was going to Yoshi Industries in Merrysville."

"Of course there are no big companies in Vancouver. You were literally just passing by, weren't you?"

"And you?"

"I'm a small time gal with a boring life. I'm in college right now and not sure of my major. I was thinking theater, perhaps, but I never thought I'd make it big or anything, so I wasn't sure it was worth the trouble. I know I'm no Gwyneth Paltrow or Sharon Stone or anything like that. I'm not model gorgeous, but, don't know."

"You're very beautiful. You just don't see it."

"Maybe, but even so, I still have no connections or anything. Hell, I don't even have any friends. Well, I have acquaintances, people I work with and all, but I'm not close to anyone, really. And I've only had a few relationships. There were a couple of guys my senior year in high school and one in college. I didn't even really like them. I just went with them because they asked."

"Maybe," Fox said, "this whole adventure happened for a reason." He leaned over and looked up at her longingly.

"And why would that be?"

"To show us both what is truly possible." He placed a hand on her shoulder and pulled her to him. Their lips met and Fox rolled her on her back, their lips never parting. He rolled over and lay on top of her body. The kiss deepened. Passion overwhelmed both of them. Fear and love came rushing out of their hearts as their hands wandered. They were lost in each other, and finding each other in the wanton throes of lust.

Joely came walking into the room.

She watched for a few seconds, unmoved by the lovers in their passionate embrace. She closed the door and decided to go explore on her own. As Joely crept around the dark, quiet house, she felt strange. In a way she was slightly jealous that Fox and Téa clung to each other for support. But she'd always put up a tough exterior because she didn't want to appear to need anyone. Despite being strong spirited, Joely was scared.

It didn't take long for Joely to wander down to the basement and find the door to the outside. She stepped out into the cool woods and smiled. She drew in a deep breath and stared at the moon. She felt free, so free it was tempting to just leave then and there, but she knew it wouldn't be fair to the others. She explored a way into the woods before heading back to the bedrooms, hoping Fox and Téa were done and she could talk to them.

Clothes had come off of both Fox and Téa as soon as Joely left the room. They didn't care if anyone saw or if anyone knew. They wanted each other desperately and needed each other for comfort. Making love in their captor's house somehow made it all the more thrilling. Fox found his way inside of Téa and began slow rhythmic thrusting. All Téa could do was feel the warm waves of ecstasy wash over her. She bit her lip to keep from screaming as the tension built up inside of her. Had any man ever made her feel this good? She didn't think so. Fox had never wanted to truly make the other woman happy and pleasure her like he wanted to do to Téa. He whispered without hesitation, *"I love you."*

Surprised he felt the same way, she said, "I love you, too."

They came to their climax as Joely was climbing the stairs back to first floor. They pulled away from each other and rested. After a few moments, they heard Joely's footsteps in the hallway outside their door. They hastily reached for their clothes and scrambled to put them back on.

There came a light knock at their door. Joely waited a moment and then entered. She shut the door behind her and said, "I found a way out."

"The door in the basement," Fox said pushing his hair back into place.

"Yeah, I explored some outside. The highway isn't very far away, maybe five minutes or so at most."

Téa asked, "Are we walking or stealing a car."

Fox clucked his tongue and shook his head. "We should try to avoid becoming criminals ourselves and walk."

"I don't think we're far from anything here. It just looks secluded. There are a few houses around and the highway."

"Should we leave now?" Téa said.

"I think we should wait a while longer and make sure everyone is out cold. Then we meet back at the door in ... like an hour. Sound good?"

Fox and Téa both nodded.

There was a brief, tense silence and then Joely spoke again. "Look, I know what happened. I came in as you guys were about to do it. I just wanted you to know that you don't have to keep a secret or anything. It's cool."

Téa let out a sigh, "Good. I didn't want you to be mad or uncomfortable or anything like that."

"Why would I be mad? It isn't like Fox and I are married or anything. We just met. Of course the two of you just met, too, but, anyway, not to change the subject. We should find the nearest police station and turn these guys in. We should tell them as much as we know."

"What do we really know," Fox said. "I mean we don't even know the last names of Paul, or Jake, or Brad, for that matter."

"Luder," Joely said. "Jake's last name is Luder."

"How did you know that," Téa asked.

Joely smiled. "Nora was calling out his name earlier. She said certain things over and over like: You are such an animal Jake Luder. I love you Luder." She shivered at the thought and laughed.

"Okay," Fox said, "so we have one name, and we can get the address off the house on the way out."

"I still find it impossible to believe that Jake has just let us to wander around the house so freely. He doesn't seem to care if we escape," Téa said.

"He's relying on our fear," Fox said. "He's counting on us to be afraid of him coming after us if we report him."

"I suppose," Téa said, "but it seems a little weird to me. I mean in all the movies and news stories you see where the captor always ends up killing his hostages."

"Aren't you a ray of sunshine," Joely said and added, "just be happy Jake isn't a typical thug and get on with it."

CHAPTER 5

They rested some and, at two a.m., they crept out of their room and downstairs. Joely paused to look at the content of some of the boxes.

"What are you doing?" hissed Fox.

"Looking for something we could use."

Fox and Téa waited impatiently for her at the door. Joely knocked something off the shelf. It was plastic, but it still made a substantially loud noise in the otherwise complete silence of the night. She snatched something from the box and ran to the door. Someone switched on the basement light and was making their way downstairs as the three of them fled into the woods.

"Who's there?" Brad said as he searched the shadows for the source of the noise.

"Shit," Joely cried as Brad reached the open basement door.

Brad pulled out his gun and shot blindly at the people moving in the dark woods. Joely turned and shot back at Brad with the gun she'd found in the box. Brad was nicked on the arm. As Téa, Fox and Joely reached an open field beyond the woods, Jake, Nora and Paul joined Brad downstairs to see what the commotion was.

"There was a break in and he shot me! He fucking shot me!" a pissed off Brad said.

They helped Brad up the stairs and into the bathroom. Jake cleaned up the wound, which was little more than a scratch. "Why would someone break in here," Jake asked Brad.

"Some drug dealer looking for money?" Brad shrugged, "Fuck, I don't know."

Jake looked up with a sudden realization. "Where are the hostages? Where are Téa, Fox and Joely?"

"In their rooms, I assume," Nora said.

Jake went to see and found their rooms empty, no sign of them anywhere. "Fuck," he muttered to himself.

"What," Paul asked coming up behind Jake.

"They're gone. It was them making the noise as they escaped. Damn Brad! He's such an idiot!"

"I am not," Brad called from the bathroom.

Jake yelled, "Nora."

Nora emerged from the bathroom in her green slip of a night gown. "What?"

"Put on your clothes. We're going to follow them."

"Well, you shouldn't have left them alone."

"Maybe not, but I didn't think they'd just leave like that. But they did. Nora, you need to go the police station and see if they're there making a report on us. We need to know what we're up against and stay one step ahead of them at all times."

"What will you do?"

"I am going to visit Bones and then leave. Call me and let me know what's up when you get there."

Nora went back into the bedroom and got dressed. She picked up her cell phone and keys and then left. Nora was far from happy with Jake and his stupid hostages. She was feeling like she wanted to kill Jake for screwing things up so badly. As usual, though, Nora would do as she was told and not ask too many questions. She took her Acura while Jake, Paul and Brad piled into the Blazer. They left moments apart to chase after the escaped hostages.

***

Once at the edge of the woods, Téa stopped to catch her breath. "I can't believe you did that Joely. You shot him."

"I know," Joely said putting her hand to her head. "I … I … wow, I would have never thought I could do something like that." She looked up with a hint of a sly smile on her face. "But you know what? It was kind of cool."

"He could have killed us."

"But he didn't."

"We're all right" Fox said, "so let's drop it. It's time to find the police station."

They made their way stealthily through the field to the highway, which they followed toward downtown. Tired and cold, it took them hours of wandering around neighborhoods to find downtown and the police station, which was closed They went around the back of the building, rested their backs against the brick wall and decided to catch some sleep until the department opened while taking turns on lookout as the other two slept. It wasn't long before all three of them had dozed off. As the sun rose that morning they woke to the sound of cars approaching and activity. They went in as soon as the doors opened and walked up to the desk.

"We'd like to make a report," Fox said to the woman at the front desk.

"Who do we talk to?" Joely asked her.

"Deputy Conley is the one on duty. Let me see if he's available." She stepped back from the desk and went through a door to a back room. She came out a few minutes later and said, "He'll be with you in a few moments. Please, have a seat."

The three exhausted former hostages sat on a hard bench across from the reception counter. Téa put her head on Fox's shoulder. Joely stretched out on her own side of the bench. They had nearly drifted back to sleep when a slightly overweight, balding man in his thirties called to them and signaled to come with him. They jumped up and followed him to a back office where they took reports. Deputy Conley motioned for them to go into the room, followed them in and shut the door behind him. He indicated seats for them to take on one side of a table. Téa and Fox sat, but Joely stood behind them. Conley sat across from them and said, "What's this report in regards to?"

"A robbery," Téa exclaimed.

"And a hostage situation," Joely added.

"Well, why didn't you say so when you first walked in? Where at? We'll send a squad car right over."

"No," Fox shook his head, "it happened two days ago,"

"In Vancouver, New York," Téa said.

"Then why are you here in Staten?" Conley said, more than a little confused.

"Because," Fox said calmly, "we—the the store we were in, Anderson Carryout—was robbed two days ago. The robber, Jake Luder, took the three of us hostage and drove us to his friend's house. We escaped from there and came directly here."

"Where is he now?"

"Still at the house—as far as we know," Joely said.

"Do you know where the house is?" Conley stopped taking notes and looked up from his notepad.

The three looked at each other and Fox said, "Somewhere here on Staten Island. It's on the beach and is an upscale place."

"East side maybe," Joely said. "We didn't get a chance to get the exact address with Brad shooting at us and all."

"Do you have any more information," Conley asked, glancing down at his report.

"Jake Luder is in his early thirties maybe," Fox said. "He's about six foot tall. His partner in crime is named Paul. We don't his last name, but Paul is a little shorter, maybe five foot ten."

Conley let out a sigh, ran his fingers through his hair, gathered his paperwork and smacked his lips. "Okay. Let me run all of this and see what I can find. I'll call you later."

Téa looked at him in disbelief. "Later? But, we haven't given you our names and addresses. And besides, none of us have phones. Not to mention the fact we don't have any place to stay in Staten. And we have no money or anything,"

The Deputy winced as he realized he hadn't gotten their names and addresses. He'd been surprised by the story and wasn't convinced it was real. Even so, as a formality and to keep up professional appearances, he took down everyone's info. When he'd finished, he said, "Let me see if I can arrange something for you, a place to stay for the day while we sort things out. Stay right here." He took his notes and left the room.

"I am *not* going to *wait*." Joely said once Conley left the room. "That jackass didn't believe us. Did you see the look on his face? He thought it was a joke."

Fox looked at her questioningly. "Where do you plan to go and how?"

Joely pulled a big wad of cash from her jeans pocket and showed it to them.

"How?" Téa said.

"While you guys were doing your thing," she winked, "I was doing mine. I'm always thinking ahead." She shoved the cash back in her pocket.

Joely opened the door and peeked out. No one was paying attention to them. The three of them walked unnoticed out of the room and through the hall to the front. As Joely pushed open the front door, Téa said, "Where do we go from here?"

Stepping outside into the morning air, Joely said, "Anywhere." "But I'd say we get a hotel room, make some calls and enjoy New York City." She descended the steps and looked around. "We can get a cab, or bus, or something back to Vancouver if you want."

"Enjoying New York City sounds good to me," Fox said and smiled.

***

Joely stepped to the curb and hailed a taxi cab. What they didn't know was that Nora had been waiting outside the station for them. She called Jake on her cell phone as she followed the taxi cab in her Acura.

"Jake here."

"It's Nora. They just left the station in a cab."

"Where did they go?"

"Don't know, but I'm following them now." Nora looked over her shoulder and changed lanes.

"Okay, keep on their tail and let me know where you end up."

"Okay."

CHAPTER 6

The cab came to a stop outside a fancy hotel in the middle of Manhattan. Joely paid the driver and they got out. Nora pulled up to the curb as the cab drove away. The three former hostages entered the hotel dressed in the same dirty clothes they'd worn for three days straight. They approached the counter much to the clerk's dismay who thought they wouldn't be able to afford this kind of establishment.

"We'd like a room," Joely said.

"You do know that rooms are three hundred and twenty-five and up."

Joely dug out several 50s and a couple of 20s. The surprised woman took the money. She handed them some papers to fill out and turned to get their key. Joely said nothing, took the key and turned to Fox and Téa. "Let's go," she said. They followed her down through the lobby to the elevator. The elevator stopped at the ninth floor. Joely ran the plastic cardkey through the door lock and the light turned green. She pushed the handle down and opened the door for them.

The room was spacious. It was immensely more elegant than the Super 8 motel they'd stayed in earlier. Téa stood still in awe as Joely strolled around and explored every inch of the room.

Téa and Fox sat on the couch and chilled as Joely got into the wet bar, helping herself to a Pepsi, candy bar and tiny bottle of whiskey. They all let out a big sigh since now they truly felt free.

"Oh, this is nice," Fox said. "I could live here."

"If only I'd gotten all their money, or at least all of the money they stole from Anderson Carryout, then we could live here for a few days at least."

"We should call home," Téa said. "I'm sure our families, at least mine, will be relieved that we're safe." While Joely and Fox chatted, Téa picked up the phone and called home.

"Hello," Téa's mom, Ruth, said.

"Mom, it's me Téa."

"Oh, thank God," she said with a gasp, then said in rapid succession, "where are you? Are you okay? They didn't hurt you did they."

"I'm fine. I'm in New York City."

"How did you get there? I thought they'd taken and killed you for sure."

"We were taken hostage and the guys drove us to New York."

"And they just let you go?"

"No, we escaped."

"You should have waited for the police. You could have been killed!"

"Mom, the police had no idea where we were."

"Have you called them? That son of a bitch should be arrested."

"We talked to some local cops, but they didn't believe us. We're going to come back tomorrow morning and talk to the Vancouver police."

"I'll call them for you."

"That's nice, but we're still going to have to talk to them."

"True," Ruth said. "I'm just glad you're alive. I cried and cried the past couple days."

"Me, too. I'll be home soon."

"Get here as soon as you can."

"I will, but we need to rest first." There was a short pause. "I gotta go. Goodbye."

"Bye."

After disconnecting, Téa sat for a moment before announcing, "I'm going to take a shower." No one said anything as she walked into the bathroom. Joely was too busy ordering room service for all of them to care and Fox was watching a baseball game on TV.

It felt like the middle of the night, but it was only noon. Jake started dozing off during the game, but was awakened by room service knocking on the door. Once Téa had gotten out of the shower, they ate and then all three of them took a long nap. Téa slept in Fox's arms and Joely slept in the other queen size bed.

As they slept, Nora waited outside, listening to Jake, who had called again. Jake was outraged and unsure if he could regain control of the situation. He instructed Nora to stay put, so she impatiently waited for Jake to make his appearance. When Jake arrived, he took Nora into a near-by "family restroom," locked the door and they did some lines before planning how to get the hostages back.

The threesome awoke around nine p.m. Joely went for a swim at the hotel pool and Fox and Téa ended up making mad passionate love. They couldn't get enough of each other. Once they'd finished and were resting in each other's arms, they talked while cuddling.

"You know," Fox said, "I could get used to this."

"Me, too." Téa sighed as she caressed his bare chest. She leaned up and her lips met his in yet another long kiss.

When she pulled away, Fox said, "One thing. What happens when this is all over?"

"I don't know. I hadn't really thought about it."

Fox nodded, understanding. "Is this the end or do I go home to visit my relatives? Or do we take a huge leap and move in together? Is this a relationship or a fling? I don't know."

"I do hope it turns into a relationship, but moving in together this soon seems a little drastic, don't you think?"

Fox shrugged. "Crazier things have happened."

"Why don't we both move somewhere together far, far away from our old lives?"

"That would be nice, but what about your family?"

"Mom would survive. This whole ordeal has made me see I was afraid of change and that I was largely unhappy with my life. I want to be free and live like Joely."

Fox smiled and stroked her breast. "And you should be free."

There was a brief knock and Joely came in. Fox and Téa shut the door between the two small rooms and dressed in a hurry. Their conversation was cut short and nothing was decided.

"You ready to go?" Joely said, coming into the bedroom now that the door was open.

"Ready to go where?" Fox asked.

"To the Asylum. It's a club my new friend Rick told me all about. It's the coolest and they play all the underground Gothic stuff you could want. They have a killer dance floor and the best drinks, I'm told. Everyone, including Madonna, hangs out there."

"I kinda want to head back to Vancouver," Téa said.

"We will, later tonight if you'd like. Let's just have some fun before we go back."

Téa sighed. "Well, I guess."

"When have you ever let your hair down? When have you ever done anything crazy? Well, besides sleeping with Fox?"

"That would be about it," Téa admitted.

"And why?"

"I just ... I don't know. I just get scared and I freeze. I'm uncomfortable with new things."

"Look Téa, you're a pretty happening chick and I happen to like you. But if you'd just learn to let go and go with the flow, you'd be a lot cooler." With that, Joely kissed Téa full on the lips. It took Téa totally by surprise. Fox laughed as Téa staggered back. Joely kept her cool and didn't miss a beat. "So what do you say? To the club or not?"

"Sure," Téa said with a laugh.

"Didn't know you were into that?" Fox said as he pulled Téa close to him again and put his arm around her.

"Is that all you men think about is beer and lesbians?"

"Yep." Fox smiled.

Téa shook her head and then the three of them proceeded to get ready for a crazy night. They left the hotel as if the entire world was theirs. As they strolled out of the front door, Jake and Nora followed them. Fox, Téa, and Joely hopped into another cab The Acura, with Nora and Jake, pulled off after them with Paul and Brad following. Both vehicles kept tabs on the cab as it darted in and out of the berserk New York City traffic. Horns honked constantly as everyone cut everyone else off.

The cab came to a stop in front of a club. Nora parked a little ways down the road from the entrance to the club and so did Brad. The robbers and their friends got out of their vehicles Jake said he had a plan he wouldn't reveal to anyone at the moment, but he promised to explain everything later. Without any further discussion, Jake and his crew got in line for the club.

The club's exterior looked like every other building on the street—a tall old brick building. It had boarded up windows and graffiti painted on the side. There was an awning over the metal double door in the front. Overall, the club was dark and gave no clue as to the life that vibrated inside.

After a short while they made it all the way to the door. As soon as it opened they heard the deep bass rumble. Lights flashed and pulsated with the music as they entered. It was huge and packed from wall to wall.

"There's nothing like this in Vancouver, that's for sure," Téa said

"Or where I'm from, either," Fox said.

"I've been to a club like this a couple of times. They were usually a little smaller than this," Joely said. "But I think you guys'll love it."

They went over to the bar and Joely ordered a drink for herself and Téa. Joely gulped hers and motioned for Téa to do the same. She took a small taste of the sour liquid and made a face. "Bottoms up," Joely yelled and Téa swallowed the rest of her drink in several gulps. Then Joely motioned for Fox and Téa to join her on the dance floor. Fox gracefully declined to dance, but sat with a view of the girls dancing together.

Joely started getting into the groove immediately, her arms and hips swaying with the beat. Téa, who'd never danced in public, tried to mimic her. It felt incredibly awkward at first, but after a few minutes the drink kicked in and she felt looser. Joely smiled at her as she got into the music and the dancing. Fox mused how the two of them were like stars shining in the dark crowd of other dancers.

Jake and Brad had made their way into the dance club as well and had spotted Jolie and Téa dancing. Joely moved to one side and then Téa the other. As the beat continued, Téa stopped mimicking Joely and began to fall into a rhythm of her own, creating a sort of routine with Joely. Joely thrust her hips and then chest before spinning around. The two women danced like they had been best friends all their lives. Their rhythm was intimate—like they were lovers on the dance floor. Téa felt as liberated on the dance floor as she had in bed with Fox. It was a similar feeling, yet still new to her.

The dance ended and Joely let out a scream and hugged Téa. "That was great," she yelled. Téa just laughed. They started off the dance floor to rest and get another drink. Téa excused herself to use the restroom. She walked past the long bar and down a dim hall to the Ladies room. She splashed water on her face since she was hot and flushed. It had been ages since she did anything that untamed or that physical. What a work out! She thought maybe she should dance more often. She closed her eyes and thought, I can't believe this has all happened to me, that I'm actually here doing these things. Téa realized she did need to loosen up and have more fun. It made her much happier than being her normal neurotic self. When she opened her eyes she saw Nora in the mirror standing behind her.

Téa jumped. "What do you want?"

"What does anyone want," she asked philosophically. "Money? Security? Sex?"

Téa turned around. "No, what do you want from *me*?"

"I want you to just disappear, but it's not me you have to worry about. It's Jake. He's upset that you left without saying goodbye."

"He didn't let us say goodbye to friends and family before he dragged us on this wild goose chase or whatever this is."

"Goose chase? Look, he just wants to talk to you. Give him that much. We're in a public place. What's the worst that could happen?"

Reluctantly, Téa followed Nora out of the bathroom and to where Jake and Brad were. She didn't ever want to see Jake again, but, for some reason, she felt obligated to talk to. She found his charm both attractive and repulsive. What was it about him? Nora led her to a private room that appeared to be riddled with bullet holes. Jake was relaxing with a beer in one hand and a cigarette in the other. The music pounded in the background and suddenly Téa felt a headache coming on.

"How nice to see you," he bellowed above the music.

Téa stepped deeper into the dark room and Nora shut a door behind her. They could still see the dancers through a panel of glass on the wall opposite the booth. "What do you want," she asked loudly.

"You have something of mine," Jake said, blowing out some smoke.

"What?"

"Money."

"What do you care? It was only like a fourth of what you stole from Anderson Carryout. Some of it is what I actually *earn* for a living."

Jake took a swig from his bottle and said, "More important than the money is your loyalty. I need to make sure you aren't going to rat me out."

"What are you afraid of? Jail? Finally get what's coming to you?"

Jake stood and walked around the table to Téa. She watched him nervously. "You've been taking lessons from Joely. You've developed quite an attitude." Jake laughed and took a long drag from his cigarette.

"What are you going to do?"

Jake looked her, "You're wondering if I plan to kill you, aren't you?"

"What can you do? Take the whole club hostage? You want to avoid a scene. You could kill me now, quietly in this room, and when I'm found I'd be a message to Fox and Joely. You would be telling them not to mess with you, but killing me could have the reverse effect. They may come after you to avenge my death."

"True," he said taking another swig of beer, "Very true. What do you suggest?"

"Oh, I would suggest you leave us alone."

"But I trusted you and you betrayed me, Téa. You and your friends told on me, didn't you?"

"Whatever do you mean?"

"You and your friends paid a visit to the police station today."

"How did you know that?"

"Nora followed you. Tell me, are the cops on my tail now? Am I a wanted man?"

"What do you think?"

"I think," he said directly into her ear, "that they didn't believe you."

"Of course they did. They went to Brad's place, but you weren't there to be picked up."

"Regardless, you betrayed me." He pulled his gun out of his leg holster, pointed it at Téa and cocked it.

Téa's heart was pounding. Was this her time? Was she going to die without anyone knowing or caring? She took in a deep breath to calm herself.

Jake touched her with the gun, but didn't shoot. "You deserve a bullet in the chest." The feel of the cold steel against her bare skin felt odd. "But it is such a lovely chest. I know Fox thinks so."

Téa was hurt and she felt like Jake was violating her with his words and his intentions. He was mocking the genuine connection between her and Fox. She felt a surge of indignation, clenched her fists and spat out, "Fuck you."

"Ah, I see we've hit a sore spot. Are you pissed at him for fucking and leaving you?"

Téa tried not to show her emotion, but the pain was apparent in her eyes. She was surprised Jake knew her deepest emotions and was now using them against her.

"You didn't think I knew, did you?" Jake continued on, taunting her. "I heard you guys in the bedroom. You were right next to us. And I wasn't blind. I saw how you clung to him like he was your life. What are you going to do without him now that he isn't here to comfort you? You know, he's probably already moved on and is fucking Joely right now."

Her anger boiled over into raging strength. She flew at Jake, fists flying and managed to hit him several times. Instead of shooting her, he let the gun cock back and dropped it to the floor. He caught her flailing arms and stifled her assault. "Damn you! You fucking sonofabitch," she screamed above the roar and pound of the music.

Jake only smiled and held her arms still and until she stopped struggling. On impulse, he pulled her closer and crushed his lips upon hers. Despite her intense anger, she found herself responding to the kiss. Jake's tongue separated her lips and tasted the inside of her mouth. His hands let go of her arms and wandered until they came to rest on her small, but firm breasts. Téa felt his hardness press against her and she hated him again—this time for stirring some hidden desire inside her. He pulled away and said, "Are you ready to co-operate now?"

She fought to catch her breath. "What exactly do you want? You need to spell it out."

"Isn't it obvious?" he said picking up his gun and placing it in her side. "Let's get out of here."

He opened the door and Nora turned from her post. "You got the money?"

"No, Joely has it. I'll take Téa to my place. You tell Fox and Joely to meet us out there or Téa gets it. Make sure they know that if they involve the police or anyone else that she dies."

Nora seemed stunned by his statement and the seriousness of his plan. "Go," Jake told Téa as he pushed her out the door. She stumbled and caught herself. They watched as Nora made her way over to Fox and Joely, then Jake pushed Téa down the hall to a back door. They exited out into the alleyway where Brad was waiting.

"You've got a thing for back doors," Téa said.

"In more ways than one."

"That's more than I needed to know."

"Have you ever gotten it up the ass," Jake asked as they headed toward the Blazer.

"No, nor do I ever plan to," she snapped. "Not that it's any of your damn business."

"Don't knock it until you've tried it," he said dragging her into the Blazer.

Jake made Téa climb in the driver's side and then crawl over to the passenger side, started the vehicle, and drove away.

CHAPTER 7

Joely saw Nora coming toward her. "Bitch," Joely screamed. She knew immediately that something had happened to Téa. She'd been gone way too long. "What did you do to her?"

Nora shrugged a shoulder nonchalantly. "Jake has her."

"Where?"

"I will take you to her if you give us the money and promise not to say anything more."

Joely snorted and stuck out her chin. "Too late!"

Nora yelled above the music. "Your visit to those clueless police officers did shit and you know that. It's your money and your silence or your precious Téa."

Fox had been listening in silence up until that point, but then he said, "You'd better not lay a finger on Téa!"

"I haven't done anything to her, but I can't promise you that Jake won't do something."

"Fine, take us to them. We don't care about the fucking money," Fox snapped.

"I can take you there, but I don't know as though Jake will be happy with your attitudes."

Nora led them out the front door and down the road to where she'd parked. Paul was waiting in the car. "So we meet again," he said to Joely as she slid in the back seat next to him.

"Shut up crackhead," Nora snapped.

"Its cokehead," Paul corrected her.

"Whatever," Nora said.

Fox jumped into the passenger seat and they drove away from the club. The half hour drive was silent for the most part and particularly uncomfortable. It felt like it lasted half a century instead of half an hour.

***

Jake had arrived back at Brad's house well ahead of the others, taking the back way and speeding most of the time. His recklessness had Téa petrified the whole time.

They arrived at a small apartment in a crappy neighborhood. Jake led Téa up the stairs to the fifth floor. They wandered down a maze of hallways until they came to a door at the end. Jake unlocked the door and shoved Téa inside. Téa caught herself from falling again and walked over to the couch. She sighed and sat, fearing what was to come next. Jake shut the door and locked the deadbolt. Then he jumped onto the couch and tried to kiss Téa. She pushed him away, but he came back, knocked her over on the couch and began groping her. It was far from subtle and Téa wasn't sure she wanted it and yet, she was strangely turned on. Jake was on top of her, tugging and ripping her clothes.

As Jake kissed her neck, she said, "Jake. We can't."

"Why not," he asked, sliding down and kissing her exposed breasts.

"Need I remind you that you are an armed robber who held me hostage? It would be improper for us to get involved."

"Live a little," he said, taking her nipple in his mouth and tugging at it. He slid down and let his tongue find its way inside of her. As ripples of ecstasy took her over, Téa forgot about who he was and how angry she was at him. Nothing mattered except how good it felt. After she came, Jake mounted her and began pushing his way inside her. Téa called out as she quivered and quaked with pleasure. She screamed and scratched his back violently as he came inside her. Téa felt like she'd completely lost control of herself and was unable to stop. Jake collapsed on top of Téa and, except for their labored breaths, there was complete silence. They didn't stay like that for long. A loud pounding came at the door, "Jake. Open up Jake."

Jake pulled out and jumped up. He grabbed his clothes and pulled them on, all the while yelling, "Just a goddamn minute." He eventually opened the door to an aggravated Nora.

"What took so long?" Nora wanted to know as they all entered the apartment. Nora suspected Jake had seduced Téa or had forced her, but said nothing.

"I was in the can. What's the hurry, anyway?"

"Where's Téa" Fox said, pushing past Nora to inspect the apartment.

"Here," she said standing up. She'd managed to pull her clothes back on before Jake had opened the door, but she still felt naked. Guilt stabbed at her as if she'd cheated on Fox with Jake. She had to remind herself that she and Fox had just met and weren't exactly a couple, though there was that potential.

Fox rushed to her side, "Are you okay? Did he hurt you? Attack you?"

"I'm fine." She sighed, sitting back down on the couch.

Fox sat beside her. "You look like you've been struggling," he said touching her tangled hair.

"If he touched you, I kill the cocksucker. Just tell me."

"I'm fine," she said squirming and fidgeting with her hair. "Really. Let's just get to the point and get out of here. He wants the money Joely stole from him."

The door was shut and locked once everyone was inside. Joely stepped from the door toward the couch. "Why should I give you the money? You have no control over us. What do we have to lose really? Nothing."

"You can lose Téa," Jake reminded her, "or you can lose your life." He turned to Joely and finished, "Or you can lose your control and let me have my way."

"Fuck you." Joely got right up in Jake's face. "You are just an immature little boy playing with big boy toys.

Jake's eyes blazed as he stared Joely down. Joely was considerably shorter and smaller than Jake, but there was a fierceness about her.

"Just let him have his way," Téa coaxed.

Joely glared at Téa. "Whose side are you on anyway?"

"Ours, of course, but it is all a game to him and it isn't worth it."

"Perhaps you are right Téa," Jake said. "But if it's all a game, what does that make you?"

"A pawn," Téa said, "But pawns can take the King in chess." She remembered what her father had once taught her about playing strategic games like chess. Although taking the King meant the game was over, it was the Queen who was considered the most powerful piece. In this case, she reasoned that Joely was the Queen and it was good to have her on their side.

"What's your strategy?" Jake asked while the others listened with considerable confusion.

Téa smiled. "I wouldn't tell you if my life depended on it."

Jake regarded her for a moment. "How do I know you won't turn me in or that the damage hasn't already been done?"

"No matter what you do you can't erase the fact that you suddenly turned our lives upside down and took our control away from us. There aren't just the legal ramifications, but the emotional ones as well. Did you ever take into account what we felt? What we wanted? Did you ever care about anyone besides yourself?"

"W-well, um, I … I."

"No you didn't." Tears threatened to free themselves from her eyes. She blinked them back. "Take your money and your control; I've had enough of this game. It was fun for a moment, but it's no way to live."

"Only a moment?" Jake said, insulted. He thought the sex had been great and that she'd enjoyed it as much as he had. Had she faked it just to make him happy? Had she duped him and lied to him as he had her? Or was it all a part of her game? He didn't know any more. Jake collected himself and said "You can go if you want, but I will hunt all of you down and kill you if the police come after me. You understand?"

"What kind of threat is that?" Joely asked. "You have no power over us."

"But I have a gun," Jake said, reaching for where he'd set it on the kitchen counter. He felt his ego deflate and sense of control fade.

"So shoot us," Joely yelled. She walked up to Jake until the only thing between them was the gun pointed at her forehead. "I dare you."

Jake stood motionless. The truth was he didn't want to shoot anyone. He didn't want to go to jail, either. He didn't know what to do.

"You don't have the balls," Joely snarled.

"And you don't know when to shut up."

"I've had it!" Téa stood even though her legs were still unsteady. Between the wild sex and the intensity of the moment, she felt more than a little weak-kneed. Still, she walked toward the door confidently as everyone watched her.

Joely rushed after Téa when she opened the door and disappeared. "Téa," she cried down the hallway, but Téa didn't stop. Joely took off after her with Joely and Fox following her lead. Téa took the stairs two at a time and scrambled to the bottom floor. She heard Fox and Joely running down after her, but paid no attention. Jake, Paul, Brad and Nora chased after Fox and Joely.

Téa exited the building and raced down the street as Joely called to her, "Téa! Come back here!"

Unable to catch up to her, Joely hailed a cab and hopped in. Fox jumped in, too, before it pulled away from the curb. Jake, Paul, Brad and Nora were left to try and catch them all on foot.

The cab pulled alongside Téa, who was still power-walking down the street. "Téa!" Joely called from the rolled down window of the cab. "Will you stop? Get in here already!"

Téa sighed, stopped and decided to get in the cab after all. The driver came to a complete stop, she slid into the back seat and Joely motioned for him to keep going.

"Where to?" the driver said.

"JFK airport," Fox said.

"That was *amazing,*" Joely told Téa. "You just up and left. That was ballsy."

"I feel horrible."

"It'll be all right," Fox said, hugging her with one arm.

Fox and Joely talked about what had happened, but Téa remained silent. She looked out the window at the busy city passing her by. When she let Jake have his way with her she'd given up her control and that made her feel demeaned. She destroyed all that she believed in. True, it did go along with Joely's whole *go with the flow* attitude, but she felt so manipulated and used. It was as if her life didn't have any meaning any longer. She always assumed she'd get married and have kids and all of that, but now it all felt pointless. She had been holding out for love, but she didn't know if she'd ever truly find it. Fox could possibly been that love she was looking for and she messed that up. If he knew what she'd done, he would never forgive her for those few minutes of passion and the thrill of danger. She'd pushed herself over the edge and now she was free falling. Her actions were coming back to haunt her. She felt she was damned.

Jake was not going to let them go that easily. He hopped into the Blazer with Paul and Brad to give chase, waving to Nora to get in, too.

Nora said, "Nope, I'm not in on this insanity this time. You're on your own."

Jake waved goodbye and then took off after his escaped hostages. He knew exactly where they were going and headed directly toward the airport.

Nora went back inside and turned the TV on to relax. She popped open a beer and decided she didn't care if Jake got himself killed. He wasn't worth worrying over.

Jake weaved in and out of traffic like a mad man. He cut off a number of people and caused two cars to collide as he sailed through a red light in an intersection. He turned down a one-way street trying a short cut. He passed by a number of one way signs, but ignored them all. He squealed his tires as he turned off the runway road and caught up to the cab on the main road. Jake pulled alongside the cab and looked over to make sure he had the right one. He did.

"*Shit,*" Joely said, "It's Jake." She pointed over at him to show Fox and Téa.

Fox tapped the cabbie's shoulder and shouted, "Floor it."

The cab shot ahead of the Blazer. Jake pulled out his gun and stuck it out of the window. Driving with one hand, he fired at the cab and missed. The Blazer swerved and Paul had to grab the wheel as Jake shot off another round. The back window of the cab shattered. The three escapees ducked in time, but there were shards of glass laced in their hair and all over their clothes. The driver yelped in fear and fury; the bullet had killed his radio.

"Now, I'm pissed." The cab driver was seething as he slowed enough to allow Jake and the gang to come alongside, yanked on the wheel sideways and rammed into the side of the Blazer. The Blazer was pushed over the yellow line into oncoming traffic. Honking horns and cussing from shouting irate and panicked drivers filled the air they tried avoid the Blazer. Jake snatched the wheel and whipped the car back over to the right side of the road, avoiding any collisions. The cab driver cut a number of oncoming cars off in order to swerve across a one-way section of road and onto an onramp for the highway. Jake followed him across the one-way section of road and was hit by three different cars, one after the other, as the car slammed and careened around in a deadly three-hundred and sixty degree demolition dance. The Blazer wasn't going anywhere any time soon.

Joely screamed for joy as they merged into the highway traffic safely. "That was fucking awesome. Great job dude!" she told the cab driver.

"It was a fucking miracle," Fox exclaimed. "They should show that on *World's Scariest Police Chases*."

"But it wasn't the police chasing us," Joely said.

"True. The police wouldn't be stupid enough to shoot at us and cut across a one-way street, either."

Téa wasn't feeling the excitement from the car chase. She'd rather have been hit by a car so someone could put her out of her misery. Death suddenly seemed inviting to her.

The cab continued peacefully on its way to the airport. He dropped them off at the front of JFK; they got out, thanking him profusely and giving him an extra four hundred dollars toward the damages done to his vehicle. The cab sped away as they went inside to buy their tickets.

Jake had fled the scene of the accident before the cops could find him. He stole a parked car on the side of the road and continued on his way with Paul to the airport. He arrived about twenty minutes after his escaped hostages did. Jake hid his gun in the bathroom, realizing he'd never get past security with it. By the time they got through the long line at the security check point, the plane to Buffalo had already left.

"Damn," Jake sighed. A moment later he added, "Fuck." Silence ensued and then he tagged on, "Shit." After a few bewildering minutes, he turned to Paul. "I guess I'll see when the next flight is. Why don't you sit down while I talk to them?"

Jake discovered the next flight to Buffalo wasn't until the next day. The Buffalo airport was not an international airport and didn't handle too many passenger flights, so their options were limited. Jake fidgeted and looked around as he tried to decide what to do next. There were no direct flights to Vancouver and not very many airports close by. The closest airport to Vancouver was a municipal airport, but they only handled freight and supply deliveries. That's when he saw the poster for Mexico. He asked the girl at the counter about it.

"We do have a plane departing for Mexico City in fifty minutes and there are still seats available. Would you like me to book them for you?"

"Yes, one ticket to Mexico City," he decided aloud. *Why the hell not*? He thought. He had nothing to lose by letting Téa, Fox and Joely go. He still had some money and it was probably best to get as far away as possible from the scene of the crime. There was a good possibility if he stayed in New York he'd eventually be picked up and thrown in jail. He couldn't shoot Téa or that bitch Joely now, so why not just leave like they did. Why not escape? Jake took his ticket and boarded the plane to Mexico without ever telling Paul and Brad.

Brad and Paul didn't see Jake board the plane. They were still waiting for Jake when the plane took off. Finally, they realized Jake wasn't coming back for them—they'd been dumped. They didn't care too much about it. Jake was nothing but trouble for them. Paul suggested they go get drunk and forget about the past week and Brad agreed.

CHAPTER 8

Téa slept on the twenty minute plane ride home while Fox and Joely talked. It was agreed the cops would be called as soon as they landed. They needed to take care of business as soon as possible and then put the fiasco behind them. The plane landed in Buffalo and they took the second, shorter flight to Vancouver. Twenty minutes after they took off from Buffalo they landed at the Municipal Airport outside of Vancouver. There was virtually no one there. Even during the day the Municipal Airport wasn't very busy—mostly postal planes and industrial flights landing. The pilot, who flew the small charter plane to Buffalo and back, had just recently started adding the route to his schedule. He only booked one round trip a day. He told them they'd been lucky to catch him. He normally left Buffalo around four p.m., but he'd been delayed until after five that day.

Fox and Joely used the pay phone in the miniature lobby area to call the local police. The police were surprised to hear from the hostages. It had only been three days, but they'd given up looking already. Even though Téa's mom had contacted them, they weren't sure they believed her. The story was not credible. Besides, big cases like robberies and hostages were out of their league. The police had decided to contact the FBI.

The police went ahead and sent a squad car out to the airport to bring them back to the station and take their statements. It took several hours for the squad car to arrive, even though they were maybe a half an hour from town. Fox, Téa and Joely were separated this time and asked to give their reports individually. For the most part, the stories matched up and they had no reason not to believe them.

Téa's mom was called to come pick her up. Since Fox and Joely had no family in town, the Sheriff put them up at a local motel. Fox hugged and kissed Téa goodbye, promising to call her first thing in the morning to see how she was. Téa nodded silently and went off with her mother. Still feeling traumatized by the past few days, Téa took a fist full of sleeping pills and went right to bed as soon as she got home. Fox and Joely checked into the L&K Motel on route 39. There, they called their friends and relatives and ordered a pizza before finally falling asleep in separate beds.

The next morning Fox tried to call the number Téa had given him, but there was no answer. He wanted to swing by and visit, but he realized he didn't have her address or a vehicle to get there even if he knew where she lived. He figured there would be time.

That morning, Téa's mother couldn't wake her daughter up. Crying and shaking, she ran to the kitchen and called 911. It wasn't long before the ambulance came.

Téa was still breathing, but she would need her stomach pumped, the paramedics said. They rushed her to the local hospital and pumped her stomach before checking her in. Téa awoke later that afternoon, sore and sad. She was lying in a hospital bed with an IV attached to her and an oxygen hose tucked under her nose. Her mother was holding her hand and sitting beside her.

"Thank god, Téa, you're awake. You had me so worried. Why on earth would you do such a thing?"

"I don't know. I was just so confused and upset." She shed a few tears, even though she fought hard not to cry. "This whole thing was so crazy; the experience of being a hostage."

"Whatever happened isn't worth ending your life over. I love you and missed you so much. I just got you back and then I nearly lost you again."

"I'm so sorry. I don't know what else to say, but I *am* sorry," Téa said with a sniffle.

Téa's mom hugged her tightly and cried with her. When her mom pulled away, Téa asked her to call Fox and Joely for her. When a psych consultant came into talk with her, her mom disappeared to call her friends.

The psychologist encouraged Téa to talk freely and she let it all out. She told her about her boring everyday life and how she hadn't been that happy to begin with all the way up to being taken hostage by Jake, and then later seduced by him. She explained her intense feelings for Fox and how she admired Joely and how she felt she'd betrayed them by having sex with Jake. She finished by saying, "I just felt so out of control. I felt like my life wasn't my own and it scared me so much."

"Well that is quite a normal reaction," the doctor said, "You already had a lot of control issues to begin with, it would seem, but you had to confront all those fears in a very direct and intense way, which made it worse for you. It's easy to see how you were overwhelmed. Still, you should have talked to someone about it rather than take such a drastic measure. I'm sure your friends Fox and Joely would have understood how you felt if you had confided in them."

"You think so?"

"Of course." Dr Mitchell smiled.

"I hope so. I feel so terrible."

"I think it might do you good to rest here for a while and then see a therapist for long term care." Téa nodded.

"You have to take things one day, one hour, one minute at a time and not worry about the future or things you can't control. Give yourself time to readjust to normal life and realize that you have changed because of this. Don't expect for everything to go back to the way it used to be. But you can embrace the change and be a better, stronger person for it."

"I just felt like my world had ended."

"But it didn't. You're still here. You still have control over so much, including how you deal with the fall out and your emotions. You always have the ability to change your attitude and actions."

Dr. Mitchell left and Téa's mom returned. She informed her daughter that her friends were on their way. Soon they were in the hospital room with her.

Fox rushed to her side and hugged her. He kissed her passionately and then pulled away to say, "I didn't believe my ears when I heard. I had no idea you were so depressed. Why didn't you say something? Didn't you know we didn't want to lose you? Why else would we have gotten you away from Jake when we could have just left you there? We care deeply about you. How could you?"

Téa started blubbering, but managed to say, "I'm so sorry. I just felt awful. Jake and I had sex and I felt like I'd betrayed both of you. I couldn't live with myself knowing that I'd willing given myself to him."

"It is okay," Fox said. "I don't blame you. He seduced you and you were in a crazy situation. Don't worry about it. Just don't ever scare us again like that. Okay?"

"But I cheated on you. I had sex with Jake and it felt good and I hated myself for it. I didn't love him. I don't know why I let him do that to me. I don't know why I didn't say no. You should hate me."

He placed a tender hand on her shoulder. "I don't hate you."

"Jake was kind of cute, in a gangster kind of way," Joely admitted.

"You aren't mad at me?" Téa looked at him, her eyes imploring deep into his.

"Well, I'm not exactly thrilled, but I'm not mad at you either. We'll get past it."

"You still want me?"

"Of course," Fox said and kissed her again. "Without a doubt."

Téa cried on his shoulder and felt much better afterward. It was as if a great burden had been lifted from her heart. Joely cracked jokes and Fox crawled in bed and lay with her for a long time before the nurses made them leave.

CHAPTER 9

Mexico City, 10 Months Later

The sun shone brightly on the shimmering surface of the pool water. It was a normal day at the apartment complex. A well tanned young man brought a drink to his to the poolside table and sat in the lounge chair. He was pretty much at ease with the life he'd created for himself. His luck had turned around and he was feeling satisfied. After all, he'd gotten away with an incredibly messy crime, until that moment.

Two other men in shorts and t-shirts were watching him. They looked at each other through their stylish sunglasses before they strode over to the man in the lounge chair. One of the men sat beside the lounging gentleman, put his feet up on the edge of the chair and smiled at him. "Thought you got away scot free didn't you?"

Jake recognized the voice. "Fox?" he said sitting up and looking at the man sitting next to him. "How on earth did you ever find me?"

"It doesn't matter. Your ass is grass and it's finally going away to jail for a long time."

"What're you going to do? Make a citizen's arrest?" Jake laughed.

"Nope, but my friend from the FBI can take you in. Duke here, "Fox jerked a thumb toward the edge of the pool, "is ready to arrest you and drag you back to the United States. You can make an unnecessary scene and embarrass yourself, or you can go quietly." He led Jake with an eye glance over to the man in black by the gate.

Duke showed Jake his gun underneath his brown jacket. Jake stood and walked quietly over to Duke. He knew his time was up and there was nothing he could do.

Fox walked along side of Jake and said, "Oh, and there's one more thing." Jake turned to ask what and met Fox's fist with his face. Fox connected with Jake's left eye and Jake stumbled backward from the force. He collapsed into a nearby lounge chair. "That's for fucking my wife!"

Uncontrollable Urges

CHAPTER 1

Lorena punched in the five digit security code and the door chirped. She put in her key and unlocked the door to the monstrosity of a modern house she called home. It was dark and quiet when she entered. Was her husband home, she wondered? Lorena didn't think so. She shut the door behind her, flicked a light switch, and checked her mail on the foyer table. Seeing nothing specifically addressed to her, she set the mail back on the table. Lorena marched up the white carpeted steps toward her bedroom. She was exhausted and longed for sleep.

Once up the stairs she went to their master bedroom suit, Lorena took off her black pumps and lay on the California King. She turned her head and the rose pattern on her comforter greeted her. Lorena reached up for one of the many pillows and pulled it to her stomach.

Where was Chad? He usually gets off work at five. But it was now ten and he should have been home. He usually didn't stay out that late even if there was a business meeting. The thought that had haunted her for weeks came back. He's having an affair. The idea made her feel like someone had punched her in the stomach. They had been drifting apart for some time. Still, the thought made her sick. Having to know for sure, she sat up and picked up the black cordless phone from its cradle. Lorena dialed his office.

"Hello," Chad said.

"Honey," she said relieved.

There was a laugh and a muffled "Shh," on the other end, and a brief pause before Chad said, "Lorena."

"I was just wondering what was keeping you there so late."

"I just had this research I had to do for a client." There was a kissing sound in the background. "It came up suddenly and I didn't have time to call you."

"That's all right."

"Look, don't worry, I'll home as soon as I finish. Okay?"

"Okay, love you."

"Bye." He hung up.

Lorena's hand shook as she eased the receiver back in its cradle. Tears were fighting to overflow. What more do I need? The proof is right there. First anger, and then sorrow, filled her. She cried for a few minutes and then collected herself. Lorena pulled herself off the bed and went to get a shower. Somehow, his actions made *her* feel dirty. After her shower she put on her sexiest black silk nightgown and fell asleep in bed, alone. The cold emptiness and loneliness of the house seeped into her heart. Then it seeped into her dreams.

CHAPTER 2

The next morning Chad was up early and getting ready for work. Lorena hadn't heard him come in the night before, so she was surprised to see him dressing as if he'd been home beside her all night. She gave him a hug and kiss even though it made her heart ache thinking about what he'd been up to the night before. In that briefest of moments they touched, she smelled the other woman on him. He hasn't even showered yet. The nerve of this man. He glided into their bathroom and shut the door behind him before she could react. The shower turned on and Lorena felt shocked and numb once again. She went downstairs and fixed herself a bagel with strawberry cream cheese. By the time he'd come downstairs to join her, her cup of tea was already cooling beside her plate.

Lorena sat on her chair and said innocently, "How did your research go?"

"Fine," he said opening up the paper.

She took a bite of bagel. "What time did you get home?"

"Uh-huh."

His apathy was beginning to piss her off. Talk was pointless, she realized, so they ate the rest of their breakfast in silence. Lorena went upstairs and got ready for work and left for the art museum. She was an art buyer and helped raise funds for the all the wonderful community activities the museum provided. Sometimes it could keep her quite busy, traveling to find new pieces to hang, arranging charity events, giving lectures and other odds and ends. It kept her occupied, but it had never kept her happy.

Later that day, Loren found herself in the home of a private art collector. He was in his mid-twenties and had inherited an insane amount of money from his now deceased parents. His father had worked hard and died young, leaving his son to play with the family fortune. Following the advice of a friend, Phillip started investing in art and sold it to make even more money. Phillip didn't have to work, so he could pursue lots of other interests

She smiled as he explained his situation and said, "I'm afraid to ask what these other interests are."

Phillip turned from the Picasso to look at Lorena. "Traveling, experiencing new sights, sounds and sensations. I like anything new, music, movies—anything in style or hot at the moment."

"Lucky you."

"Now why do you say that?" he said as they began walking down his long, open hallway.

Lorena followed him and watched as he poured himself a drink from the table in the study they'd just entered. "I don't know."

"You want a drink?"

"Sure."

Phillip poured a glass of sweet brandy and handed it to her. "Why am I so lucky?" he asked.

Lorena took a sip and said, "You are free and wild. My life is so utterly boring. I work and I go home to my husband who's never there ...." She trailed off in midsentence. She glanced around the room and noticed a wall of books, all of them unread she imagined. There was a desk and a computer in the room as well. She wondered where his gigantic TV and stereo were and why there were no personal pictures hanging up anywhere.

"Promise you won't get offended," he said.

"What do you mean?"

"I mean that you're a beautiful woman and very sweet, but you also seem unhappy. I'd like to give you a taste of my life is all and maybe then you will find a bit of happiness."

"I'm flattered, but I'm not sure."

"What are you afraid of? I won't make you do anything you don't want to."

Silently, he approached her, took the empty glass from her hand and set it on the table. His fingers glided up her arm and his lips descended upon hers. Lorena didn't fight him and she relaxed as his tongue thrust apart her lips. The kiss continued to deepen and he wrapped his arms around her. After a moment, he pulled away. "Is that what you want?" he said in a seductive murmur.

Unsure of what she wanted, she changed the subject. "We'd like to buy the Picasso. How much do you want for it?"

"Let's discuss the price later," he said taking her hand and leading her over to his desk. Phillip pushed what few papers were on the desk off onto the floor. He gestured for her to followed his lead and lay on the desk.

Lorena paused and thought about the level of weirdness going on. What? Does this guy think he's living inside some cheesy porno or something? He just expects her to do what he wants without question?

"You know you want to," he said, his tone imploring and convincing.

Lorena was stunned as she thought. I really do want to. She hadn't been with many men before she married Chad. She was his trophy wife and she'd little time to sleep around. Hell, she'd only been eighteen when they married. Emptiness had befallen her and her marriage not long after the honeymoon. She'd hoped they could have kids to fill that void, but for some reason they never did conceive. In her thirties, her biological clock was ticking away, and she wasn't so sure kids would fill that hole for her.

"Come on," he coaxed as if she were a child.

Lorena took a step toward the desk and sat on it. Phillip's hand slid up her black skirt and pulled down her black lace panties. He kissed her neck as he undid the buttons on her white blouse. She unzipped his pants and helped him free himself from the restriction of his skimpy underwear. Before they could finish undressing each other, Phillip shoved her skirt up. It shocked her that he was in so quickly and without any foreplay, but it didn't matter. She was still wet for him and he found it easy to start the rhythmic and sometimes almost violent thrusting. Lorena pushed all thoughts of her husband from her head; rationalizing he'd cheated on her many times and she deserved this one little treat.

His roughness turned her on. She found herself writhing in ecstasy as Phillip came inside of her. Lorena screamed out as she felt herself falling over the brink of rapture. She shivered and shook uncontrollably. It had never been this way with her husband—ever.

Now she saw what she was missing and she didn't feel one bit guilty about it. Lorena suddenly felt in control of the situation and as if she was the one using Phillip.

Phillip rested for a moment on top of her and the pulled himself up. As he pulled up his underwear and pants, he told her the museum could have the Picasso at low-price and if she wanted to ever have more fun, just to call him. He gave her his cell phone number and she left.

CHAPTER 3

A few days had passed and Lorena was home alone again. She called Chad's office but he didn't answer. She called the car phone and didn't get an answer there, either. Lorena was feeling more than fed up. She picked up the phone a third time—this time to call Phillip.

"Hey," he answered.

"Hey Phillip, this is Lorena Floirentino."

"Hey," he repeated with a much more interested tone.

Just a few hours later Lorena was in a cheesy motel downtown. She went to door number 26 as instructed and opened it. On the bed was a wig and lacy negligee. The note told her to put those on. As she placed the long blond wig over her long black hair, she felt rather like Alice in Wonderland. The negligee was red and just the right fit. Once she finished her wardrobe change, Phillip strolled out of the bathroom. He'd been there watching her the whole time. She smiled as he approached her, naked.

Phillip pushed her down on the bed, unsnapped the red lace bodice and placed his finger inside her. He slid down between her legs. Lorena closed her eyes and enjoyed the warmth of his breath on her thigh and inside her. When she quivered several times, Phillip mounted her.

Both were worn out, they napped. When Lorena awoke it was midnight. She pulled on her regular clothes and took off the blond wig. She kissed the sleeping Phillip good-bye and slipped out of the room. This time it was Chad who could be surprised that his wife had gotten home so late. Is he asleep, she wondered, as she as she crawled in bed next to him, or pretending? I wonder if he can smell Phillip on me? She didn't care much.

After the second rendezvous, Lorena found herself totally into this new world. The third time she called Phillip, he suggested something new and exciting for her.

"Like what?" she said. She was at work hoping nobody interrupted her phone call or overheard her conversation. She didn't want to be caught flirting. Phillip made her giddy as school girl and she didn't want others to get suspicious.

"I think we could add more people to the mix. My friends Mark and Jim would love to experience what we have and so would Amber and Nicole."

"Are you suggesting a threesome or an orgy?"

"Whatever you are comfortable with baby." He laughed. "I'm open to another guy or another woman; anybody to mix it up. Just let me know."

"I'll have to think about it," she said nervously.

"Mizz Floirentino," the receptionist called, sounding angry.

"I gotta go. Talk to you soon."

"I'll be waiting."

Lorena hung up and looked up at her twenty-something blond receptionist. For a moment, Lorena couldn't help but wonder what her sex life was like. She surprised herself by wondering what it would be like to have sex with her. Trying to keep her embarrassing thoughts to herself, she responded calmly, "Yes, Linda?"

"These papers need to be signed and Mister Morrison called. He wants to know if you can make the meeting tomorrow."

All day long Lorena thought about Phillip and his offer. She let her imagination go wild and fantasized what it would be like to have sex with another woman. Although she enjoyed the idea of the soft, gentle female touch, she decided she liked the idea of being worshipped by two men. She couldn't focus on anything related to work. All the new and exciting things she was experiencing was overwhelming her and it was difficult to keep it a secret.

That night she went home to Chad, who was there waiting for her—for once. He was sitting on the couch having a drink. The TV was on, but he wasn't paying any attention to what was on.

"Hi honey," she said walking toward him.

"Hi sweetie," he said absent mindedly.

"You're home early for once."

"Yup."

"Bad day?"

"Yup."

Lorena sat in a chair next to Chad. "Why don't you tell me about your day?"

"Not much to tell." He sighed. "I lost a client and everyone is mad. He blamed me for not telling him that stocks could and often do fall. I'm a broker," his voice raised," not a *goddamned psychic*. That Paul is a fucking moron. I hate him. I wanted to …" Chad paused.

"No need to be so angry. It's over now. You can just leave it alone and let it go you know."

"I can't, though. I'll never live this down. What will everybody think of me?"

"Who cares?"

"They do. I do."

Lorena sat back, not knowing what else to say. She hated it when he got perturbed like that. Her father used to do the same thing. She shuddered at the memory and began watching the program on TV.

Later, Chad took a sleeping pill and drank several more drinks. When he was out cold, Lorena called Phillip. He was happy to hear from her.

"What's up Lorena," he asked when he knew it was her.

"I'm guessing you are."

They both laughed. "Not yet, but I soon will be if you have anything to do with it."

"So I thought about what you said."

"And?"

"And another man sounds ideal. Perhaps later we will try another woman. There are just so *many possibilities*."

"Yes, there are and I'm so glad you're open to all of this. It's thrilling to see you open your eyes to a whole new world."

"All thanks to you."

"So when do we meet again?"

"I'm not sure." She took the cordless and began walking toward Chad's home office. There was a long pause as she found his planner and flipped through it. He had only jotted down a few things. On one of the days he wrote just one word—a woman's name, Amber. There were a couple of lunch meetings scheduled and then he was taking a brief visit to a friend's lakeside house. It was a party to celebrate something, but she couldn't remember what. He had mentioned it to her in passing. She couldn't recall what it was exactly, but it prompted her snap decision. "Friday night."

"Are you sure you can get away then?"

"My husband has a party." There was click on the other line, but Lorena chose to ignore it. After all, Chad had taken a sleeping pill. He couldn't possibly still be awake. She continued, "I was invited to go, too, but it isn't a big deal if I duck out. I don't really know any of the people. It's all people Chad knows from work."

"If you are sure."

"Yeah."

"Okay then, we will all meet at my house."

"Should I bring anything?"

"Yourself. I'll supply the rest." He chuckled.

"What time?"

"Sometime around seven p.m."

"All right, see you then. I'm looking forward to it."

"Me, too. Me, too."

***

So did Chad. He'd heard the last bit of the conversation. It wasn't enough to totally condemn Lorena, but it was more than enough to raise his suspicions. It could be something innocent, he reasoned, but why would she keep it a secret if it was so innocent? Anger boiled inside him, but he kept it to a simmer. He was going to need proof. Then, and only then, would he act. He would make her live to regret it if she was cheating. Lorena was his wife and she belonged to him. It made him feel violated just to think of another man touching her.

***

Lorena snooped around the study with the cordless still in her hand. Business books Chad had never opened lined the bookshelves. The computer sat dark and dusty on top of the desk. She remembered when he'd first gotten the computer she couldn't pull him away from it. Lorena glanced over the desk and noticed a photo of them together on their honeymoon. It had been a wonderful trip that she knew she would not soon forget. He made love to her and cherished her like she always wanted. Ten years later there were no pictures of kids, no family vacations, and no holidays. It made Lorena more than a little sad. Chad had wanted kids at first, but she had originally wanted to wait. She wanted them to spend a year alone together, but that year had gone by so fast. Then Chad had gotten ambitious and too busy with work. He'd moved up in his company and they moved from an apartment to a nice big house. They bought it with the intention of filling it with kids one day, but it had remained empty.

Her thoughts shifted back to Friday night. Hungry with desire, she decided to go to the kitchen and feed herself. She retired to bed, one night cap and an hour later. Chad was still lying in bed, sound asleep.

CHAPTER 4

Friday came. Both Chad and Lorena went off to work that morning. They arrived home after dinner time and met briefly in the bedroom while Chad was getting ready for the party.

"You ready to go," he asked as he buttoned up his shirt and tied his tie.

Lorena's heart sank. She'd been dreading this moment all week. Lies of omission were easy, but making things up didn't come naturally to her. "Oh, is that party tonight?"

"You've known about the Motola's party for over a month now."

"I completely forgot and I have this horrible migraine. Do you think they'd mind terribly if you went without me? I really need to go lie down." She sat on the bed, doing her best to look beat.

"It won't be as much fun without you."

"I'm so sorry. Maybe we can go out to dinner next week or something and I can make it up to you."

Chad nodded and came over to her. "I do wish you'd come, but since you don't feel up to it." He leaned down and kissed her lightly on the lips.

She kissed him back, briefly. "Thank you." Lorena laid down and curled up on the bed. Chad finished getting ready for the party. His kissed Lorena good bye and left. A few minutes after she heard his car pull out of the driveway, she got up and got herself ready. She put on a slinky black dress and dangly earrings. She pulled her raven hair into an up-do and touched up her make-up. Lorena usually wore fairly modest clothes, but tonight she felt like being more than a little daring. This was an outfit that Chad had picked out for her, but she'd always been too self-conscious to wear, until now. She drove away in their Lotus, happy that Chad had decided to call for a limo. Chad usually took the Lotus everywhere he went on weekends so he could show it off. The thing was ghastly expensive and he drove it like a race car driver, but he took great pride in his toy.

Lorena blasted the radio, enjoying the sense of freedom she felt that night. She sang along to Jennifer Lopez's song *Waiting for Tonight.*

She parked behind Phillip's house. When she arrived, Phillip greeted her. He offered her a drink and they talked in the white plush living room for a few minutes before heading upstairs.

Lorena had been nervous at first, but Phillip put her mind at ease and the drink helped relax her as well. When they entered the room there was a smell of incense and New Age music played softly in the background. "I hope you don't mind the music and everything." Phillip said. "Mark likes that sort of thing."

"No, no it's fine." It was hardly the kind of music she imagined having wild sex to, but she found she liked the relaxing music. It made the experience seem more tantric, more mystical.

Lorena lay on the bed next to Mark and Phillip lay on the other side of her. They discussed briefly what they wanted. Mark wanted to pretend to seduce Lorena while Phillip watched. Once they were in the middle of having sex, then Phillip would join them. She was a little unsure of anal sex, but Phillip reassured her it wouldn't be a big deal.

Phillip kissed Lorena passionately, slipped out of bed and into a comfy chair to observe. At first Lorena was distracted by Phillip's audience, but eventually Mark made her forget him altogether.

Mark began by lying next to her and caressing her face. He whispered to her how beautiful she was and how much he wanted her. His lips pressed against hers. His tongue probed her mouth. Finally, his hands reached up her dress and slid across her thighs. He inched the dress up and she pushed it back down. He grinned and kissed her neck before trying to reach around and unsnapping her strapless bra. It came unsnapped and Lorena pretended not to notice.

Again, Mark's fingers danced up her legs and reached between her legs. He pulled her lace panties off and began circling her warm moist desire with his fingers. He plunged his fingers in and out of her, feeling her grow more and more excited with each brush. He paused to play with the tiny rose bud of her clitoris. Lorena's breathing increased as she felt her heart pound in her chest. The pleasure was building inside of her rapidly and she wasn't sure she could contain herself.

Mark pulled her dress over her head and her bra came along with it. He tossed it on the floor and ran his hands over her delicious curves. He leaned down and caught her nipple in his mouth, sucking it gently. Lorena couldn't help but moan. Mark smiled and moved over to her other nipple. He played with it with his tongue for a few wonderful moments before he slipped down between her legs. Mark's tongue darted in and out of her playfully and Lorena found herself plunging over the edge of ecstasy. She writhed and wriggled with pleasure before giving into the violent shivers of pure orgasm.

When he was satisfied with her intense pleasure, he quickly undressed and put on a condom. He sunk down onto Lorena and let his hardness drive deep into her. She gasped and groaned as he started the rhythmic thrusting. She clung to his muscular arms as he shuddered with his own orgasm. Mark pulled off of her and rolled to his side. He began covering her with kisses as Phillip slipped slyly into bed with them. Lorena could feel his erection press hard into her back and rear end. He slipped his finger into her anus and began to create new sensations in Lorena. It hurt at first, but then slowly his fingering began to ignite a new fire. As Mark fingered her warm, wet vagina, Mark suddenly thrust into her.

Lorena screamed, but Mark covered her mouth his urgent kisses. Soon, Phillip was thrusting and pulling at her hips as he sodomized her. It felt like he was ripping her in two at first, but then she felt herself tremble and shake with a second orgasm. Pain and pleasure blended into one prickly hot wave of throbbing rapture.

Exhausted, Lorena lay still between Phillip and Mark. It took her a long time to be able to get up and get dressed. Her legs felt like they wouldn't hold her up as she wandered into the bathroom. She sat on the toilet to discover herself bleeding from the anal sex. She frowned and put on a panty liner before heading home. Hopefully, Chad wouldn't come close enough to ask questions any time soon.

CHAPTER 5

Lorena drove home tired, but glowing from her wild experience. She felt more alive than ever before. She'd been mostly asleep through her marriage to Chad. Their whole relationship felt defined by distance and coldness. She knew now she had always craved the passion she'd felt that night. Lorena knew she'd truly loved Chad and that was why she married him. If only she'd known what would happen to them, that it wouldn't last. Lorena pushed the button for the garage door to open and carefully parked the Lotus back in her spot in the garage. Chad was not home yet, and for that, Lorena was grateful. She went upstairs to shower and sleep.

***

Chad had not gone directly to the party. Instead, he had waited for Lorena to leave and then followed her to Phillip's house. He taken a few pictures of her and Mark together using a high tech telephoto lens on his camera and then left. He made a brief appearance at the party, ate some shrimp and drank some martinis before heading back over to Phillip's house. He was relieved to see Lorena had left. It meant Chad could go home. He crawled in bed next to a sleeping Lorena and plotted his revenge.

***

Lorena was now addicted and sex was her drug of choice. She wanted more and more. She was insatiable. When she awoke on Saturday morning she wanted nothing more than to go to Phillip's and see what new ecstasy he could bring her. Lorena prayed silently Chad found something to do that day and would leave. Unfortunately, Chad slept in longer than usual and then rolled over to greet Lorena who was awake, but still lying in bed.

"Feeling better?" he said sweetly.

"Uh, maybe a little. I think I'll stay home and take at easy, though. Why don't you get out and play golf or something today?"

They belonged to an exclusive Country Club known as Red House, but they didn't often take advantage of their membership. Chad nodded. "Good idea. I haven't been there in a very long time. It'll be nice. Maybe I'll call Doug up and see if he wants to go with me."

"Great idea."

As Chad rolled out of bed, he added, "I bragged last night at the party how I could kick Doug's ass at racquetball any time and any place. Maybe he'll be up for that as well."

"Okay," she said rolling over. "Have a great time."

Chad dressed and got something to eat before taking off for the day. He couldn't leave quick enough for Lorena. It felt like it took him forever to pull on his clothes to go to the club. When his car pulled out of the driveway, once again, Lorena snatched up the phone by her bed and called Phillip.

"Good morning," she greeted when he picked up.

"Good morning to you, too. I was calling to tell you I had so much fun last night. When can we meet again?"

Phillip laughed, "You're incredible. Can't you get enough?"

"Nope, never." She laughed back.

"I unleashed a nympho. Look out world, here comes the sex goddess Lorena."

Lorena lay back on the bed and stared up at the ceiling. "It's your fault, you know."

"Cool. Today is as good as any other. Although, I'm leaving for Japan in a week."

"I wish I could come with you."

"You can."

"My husband."

"Tell him you have a business trip or something. Create alibis by telling him you're visiting a sick relative or something and have them cover for you."

"Let me think about it."

"Okay, in the meantime, what adventure do you want for today?"

"Another woman sounds enticing."

"Perfect, I'll bring Amber over."

"Bring over?"

"Yeah. How exciting for you to have sex in your bed with someone else besides your husband. Very naughty."

"But what if he comes home?"

"That's part of the fun, the risk of getting caught."

"I suppose."

"You said you lived in Fox Run?"

"Yeah, but I don't know about this."

"Chill out. What's the worst thing that could happen? Your husband will catch you with another woman. I'm sure he'd like that idea. I know I do."

"Okay."

A few hours later Phillip and Amber appeared at her doorstep. Lorena invited them in with a smile and showed them around. Phillip seemed casual and very much at home already. Amber was quiet, but interested in everything Lorena and Phillip said. She was open to whatever was suggested. It was Phillip who came up with the idea that Amber bathe Lorena in the tub.

Phillip watched from a distance as Amber undid Lorena's button up shirt and slid it off her shoulders. Then she slid Lorena's shorts to the floor, helped her step out of her panties, ran the warm water and filled the tub.

"So how did you meet Phillip," Lorena asked as she stepped into the tub.

Amber pushed a strand of her deep red hair behind her ear and reached for a bath cube. "I met him at a hiking retreat. We had sex on the trail in the pouring rain just for the hell of it. After that he took care of me. We really depended on each other for survival on the hike." Amber turned off the water and found a soft sponge that she poured lavender scented body wash onto. She lathered it up and began to tenderly use it to wash Lorena's arms, legs and breasts. "We kept in touch, even though he lived in New York and I lived in South Carolina. A couple of months ago he introduced me to an agent who got me a great job at a modeling company. I got a fantastic job and casual sex whenever I wanted it. Fucking friends I'd guess you'd call us."

"I guess that's what Phillip and I are, too. So you model? I modeled some when I was younger, but I got out of it. Chad didn't like me being on display like that, but I loved it.

"You should model," Amber said. "You're still very beautiful."

"Thank you."

There was a long silence as Amber dipped the sponge between her legs and washed her most delicate and private spots with the greatest of love. The sponge dropped into the water and Amber let her fingers slip inside of Lorena. Lorena let out a small noise of pleasure and surprise. She closed her eyes and let herself enjoy the sensations. Whatever inhibitions she had getting into the bath were gone.

Amber withdrew her fingers and reached for a towel. She helped Lorena out of the tub and dried her off. Lorena was no longer dripping wet from the water, but she was still turned on as Amber led her to the bed. They lay together and Amber took her time caressing Lorena's face, breasts and stomach. She kissed her neck and made her way down to Lorena's already erect nipples. The ache of desire was unbearable and Lorena found it difficult to be patient as Amber took her time cherishing her.

When Amber paused, Lorena decided it was her turn. First she crushed her lips against Amber's soft pouty lips and tasted her sweetness. Lorena let her hands drift over Amber's firm ample breasts and down over her rounded ass. Amber smiled as she saw Lorena getting into it and enjoying herself. Lorena leaned down, took Amber's nipple in her mouth and sucked. Amber moaned slightly as Lorena moved over to the other breast and sucked that one as well. Lorena couldn't resist slipping her finger between Amber's legs and seeing if she was as aroused as she was.

Indeed, Lorena found Amber more than a little wet. Curious as to what Amber's desire tasted like, she slid down between her legs. She darted her tongue deep inside of Amber and tasted the nectar in all of its wonderful warmth. Amber moaned and shivered.

"Good?" Amber said when Lorena came up from between her legs.

"Uh-huh," Lorena said pressing her lips to Amber's so that Amber might taste herself.

Amber and Lorena kissed for a while longer before Amber slid down between Lorena's legs and licked her into orgasmic oblivion. Lorena thought she would die over and over again, but her heart never stopped. It just pounded in her chest the whole time she and Amber were together. Lorena had never known sex could be so intimate and intense. Being with another woman was a whole other world from being with men and Lorena decided she loved that other world now that she had visited it.

***

Phillip watched with great interest. It didn't bother him both Amber and Lorena had completely forgotten his presence. Watching others and knowing he had a hand in helping them get off was enough. Though he wouldn't have minded joining them, he could see they were already content and worn out.

CHAPTER 6

Hours later Lorena was lying out in the sun beside her pool in the backyard. Her thoughts drifted to what had transpired earlier that day. She'd never guessed being with a woman could be so satisfying or that exciting. As much as she glowed from the experience, something was still troubling her. She knew she had deceived Chad over and over again recently and she hated herself for it. Yet, it made her realize she no longer wanted to be with Chad. Leaving him at this point was going to be incredibly difficult, though. A bitter divorce could drag on for a long time; destroying them financially and emotionally.

The cordless phone rang on the table beside her "Hello."

"Lorena, it's Nikki."

"*Nikki.* I haven't heard from you in forever. How are you?"

"Great, actually. I've been really busy starting my own practice."

"So are you raking in the big bucks talking to all those crazy people now?"

"They aren't crazy. They just need help."

"So where's your new office?"

"Corner of Marion and Central. It's a beautiful place and I've already got a full case load of patients. Most of them are overflow from Doctor Moody."

"Your life is way more exciting compared to mine."

"Somehow I doubt that."

"Well, I do tend to meet the same people over and over and that means the conversation is the same one over and over as well. It gets more than a little tedious at times."

"I can imagine. How about we meet for coffee later this week?"

"Sure. When?"

"How is Tuesday at four p.m.?"

"Sounds good. Which Starbucks?"

"The one on Northline inside Barnes and Noble, okay?"

"Yeah, perfect."

"See you then."

They hung up and Lorena turned from her back to her stomach. She saw a shadow over her a few minutes later. She looked up to see Chad standing beside her.

"Hi honey," he said and smiled.

"Hi," she said raising her head to get a better look at him. "How did your game go?"

"Great. How did your day go? Did you go out at all?"

"It was good. I was too tired today to go anywhere, so I stayed here all day. It was nice to just stay here." That was the truth.

"So I didn't miss anything exciting?"

Lorena thought it a bit odd of a question, but remained calm. "Nope, nothing exciting."

Chad leaned down and placed a quick kiss on her lips.

***

Later that night they lay on the couch together and watched a movie. Lorena was surprised Chad wasn't out carousing with other women. It was sure a change from the past Saturday nights. He always claimed to have meeting with clients and all kinds of other matters to tend to. He hated staying home. Lorena tried to be content with him being home, but the truth was she really wished he would have gone out that night. She wanted to be lying on the couch with Phillip, Mark or Amber, anybody but her husband.

Lorena knew something was up when Chad cupped her breast and began kissing her neck. Her first thought was, Oh God I hope he doesn't want sex! But he did. He picked her up and carried her upstairs in a grand romantic gesture so that he might win her over and seduce her like the other men had done. Lorena kept up the façade of interest as Chad laid her down on the same spot where Amber had made love to her earlier. She ached for Amber's touch, but instead she felt the rough, callous touch of her husband. Chad began to peel away her clothes starting with her shorts and underwear. He didn't bother to take off her shirt or bra.

She turned her head and looked away as Chad mounted her. She wasn't wet or turned on in the least and it began to hurt as he kept ramming harder and harder. She wanted to push him off and tell him to stop and never do it again. Lorena cried silently as Chad finished.

"Lorena!"

"What?" she said turning to look at him.

"Why are you crying?"

"I'm just too tired and not really in the mood is all."

***

Chad rolled off of her and lay on the bed beside her. He said nothing, but Lorena knew rage was boiling just beneath the surface. Lorena didn't know he'd parked the Jeep Grand Cherokee in the small woods on the hill across from their house and spied on her. He used his telephoto lens and got a perfect view through the bedroom window. From the hill he first saw Phillip pull up in his car with Amber. He watched as Amber and his wife had sex. Although he'd grown stiff as he watched the two of them together, he also became enraged at Lorena's deception. Why did she feel the need to hide these sexual escapades? Hell, he didn't even understand why she felt the need to dirty herself by doing all of this. She had been Chad's perfect little angel, so sweet and innocent. Now she had to go and shatter that image he had of her being the perfect unsoiled woman of his dreams. Once more, Chad felt hurt, left out and out of control.

That afternoon he did go to the Red House Club with Doug and play Racquet Ball and then golf. Doug commented on how angry and distracted Chad seemed all day, but Chad denied anything was up or wrong with him.

CHAPTER 7

Tuesday came and Lorena went to work. The gallery closed early on Tuesdays so she had a short day. When she finished closing up the gallery, Lorena headed out to the Starbucks at Barnes and Noble to meet her friend Nikki. She arrived promptly at four p.m. and ordered a Cappuccino. Once she got her Grande-size cup of coffee she sat in the black chair across from her friend. Nikki had already gotten her cup of steaming hot black coffee with two sugars and no cream.

"So how have you been?" Nikki smiled. Her long blonde hair cascaded over her shoulders. Her blue eyes were wide and friendly. She was genuinely glad to see her friend.

"Not too bad."

"It has been almost a year since we've been able to sit down and talk. I saw this Monet in a gallery that was actually for sale. When I bought it to put in my office, I thought of you. I really do miss our long talks."

"I know, I miss them, too. I could have used you a few weeks ago."

"What happened?"

"Well," Lorena smiled. She leaned in and said, "promise not to tell?"

"I swear," Nikki was and sounded excited.

"I met this guy, Phillip, when I was buying art for the gallery. Anyway, we ended up *doing it on his desk.*"

"No."

Lorena laughed and waved her hand downward at her friend. "Shh, we're in a public place. But yes. And *I loved it.* Anyway he got me into this whole experimental thing and I can't stop."

"How many times have you been with him, then?"

"Oh, it was just the one time with him and only him. He introduced me to a couple of other people and I hooked up with them, too."

"Wow, I never saw you as the wild type, but I guess everyone has to break out of their shell sometime. But Chad is going to be furious if he ever finds out."

"I know, but I was kind of hoping he never would."

"If this continues, I'm sure he will. It's always difficult to keep up the lies for too long."

"I know." Lorena sighed.

"I didn't think the two of you were all that unhappy."

"Neither did I," Lorena said, close to tears.

"It's all right," Nikki comforted her.

"It's just that Chad stopped having sex with me and he was staying out late all the time. I called him once at work to see what was taking so long and I heard this woman in the background giggling. I was just hurt and lonely and fed up. Phillip really is the best thing that ever happened to me. I just don't know what Chad would do if I filed for divorce."

"You don't think he'd do anything to hurt you do you?"

"I don't know. Maybe."

"Then maybe you should get a lawyer and find a way to protect yourself."

"Chad knows all the best lawyers in town. He'd still end up with everything and I'd end up with nothing. He'd find a way to prove I'd been cheating and make him look completely clean and innocent."

Nikki's expression and shoulders sagged, she shook her head. "That's too bad. Maybe you could take a vacation and think about what your next move is."

"That's a good idea. Where would I go, though?"

"Take time off and go to San Francisco or L.A. You don't even have to go that far. Just check yourself into a hotel around here."

"What would I tell Chad? I guess I could tell him it's work related. That's always his excuse."

"Do that, then."

"I think I will. Thanks." Lorena smiled. "So, enough about me. What's up with you?"

"Not a whole lot to tell. I'm still dating this guy, Matt. We've been talking about getting married, but I don't think either of us are ready. My mother and all of my friends are conspiring against me, though. They're determined that I be married before I hit thirty."

"I wish I would have waited."

"You were young and in love."

"Eighteen was too young."

Nikki went on about her new office and some of her patients. Lorena listened with interest, but what she needed to do hovered over her like a giant storm cloud. Nikki rambled on about how great the sex was with Matt and how lame it had been with her former boss. The afternoon sped by and Lorena and Nikki left Starbucks two and half hours later.

Lorena didn't go home. Instead, she drove to Phillip's estate and talked to him about what had happened with Chad and how she was feeling. She didn't break down and cry like she was afraid she was going to. Instead, she told him, "I need some time to think about things I think. I am going to take a vacation."

"What about taking a vacation together?"

Lorena had forgotten he'd suggested that earlier. She thought for a second and said, "How about you give me your number where you'll be staying at and I'll join you later if all goes well. I can't promise anything, but would definitely like to keep my options open."

"That sounds good; although, I wish you'd just forget the old fuddy-duddy husband and run away with me."

"I know." There were no more words. Lorena straddled him on the couch and encouraged him to let his hands wander. Phillip soon had both of them undressed and in an intimate and passionate embrace. Their passion soon spilled over onto the floor and eventually the bed. It was full of energy she never knew she possessed. Chad usually was done in ten minutes and that was that, but he kept coming time and time again.

CHAPTER 8

That night Lorena went home and packed a few things. Chad wasn't home, as usual. Lorena hoped she could leave before he came back to ask a million and one questions. She wrote a note explaining how she had a surprise business trip to Boston and that she couldn't get out of. She taped the note to the hall mirror. Chad had taken the Lotus, so she took the Grand Cherokee and drove it to the Sheridan downtown and checked in. Lorena took her key card and turned to go to the elevator.

It was then she saw, of all people, Chad. He was over by the drinking fountain with a young red-headed woman who was hanging all over him. They kissed and talked loudly, not caring who saw them. She couldn't believe her eyes. *That bastard!* Lorena's heart missed a beat as she slid over to elevator and pushed the button. She prayed Chad wouldn't turn his head and see her. "Come on, come on," Lorena muttered out loud. It felt like the elevator took forever to descend and open, but it finally did. Chad and the girl started over toward the elevator as she slipped inside. She hit the button to close the door repeatedly and it shut before he looked up. Lorena let out along breath and steadied herself. Her knees had gone weak and her heart was beating fast. She had been incredibly afraid of meeting Chad because she knew he'd make her feel like shit and ruin her vacation. She realized she should have had the strength to confront him. After all, he was the one in a compromising position, not her. Yet, she knew he'd deny what was right in front of both of their eyes. And the truth was that she knew she'd cheated, too. She was no longer innocent now. But that wasn't the point. The point was she wanted to get away from Chad and everyone else so she could clear her head and figure out what she wanted.

The elevator shot up to the eighteenth floor. The doors opened and she stepped out. Still afraid Chad was going to jump out like the boogey man and yell boo, she walked nervously down to her room. Once safely in, she shut the door and fell onto the bed. She closed her eyes and let out a huge sigh of relief. Bored by the utter silence, Lorena soon flipped on the TV. She tried to relax, but the thought of Chad and the other woman haunted her. Determined to try and erase the memory, she dug into the fully stocked mini-bar and drank all the liquor inside.

***

Late that night, someone entered Phillip's house, but he wasn't silent as he broke in. A man came from the upstairs and peered down the dark hallway to see what the noise was. Before the man could determine who or what had made the noise, someone from the shadows punched him in the eye. The intruder kept hitting and kicking the man repeatedly in a burst of violent energy. He didn't stop until the man was motionless on the floor. Blood gushed from his lip and nose.

The intruder slipped away before the Sonitrol Security people responded to the triggered silent alarm. A man was found unconscious on the floor by the police and paramedics, but it was not Phillip. Phillip had already left for Tokyo, Japan. It was Mark, who was house-sitting for his friend. Unfortunately, his stay was short. He was rushed to the ER to be treated for numerous cuts, broken ribs and internal bleeding. After he regained consciousness, police came to his room to question him. Mark had not seen the face of his attacker and had no idea who might have wished him harm. The police weren't sure if Mark was the intended victim or not. While the police weren't doing much, the press, however, did do something. The story made front page in all the local newspapers: *Man Attacked At Friend's Estate.*

CHAPTER 9

Lorena woke up with the sun streaming in her window and hurting her eyes. She'd had too much to drink the night before and had a mild hangover. As she pulled herself off the bed she realized that getting drunk hadn't been a way to solve anything. She'd just succeeded in making herself more miserable than before. Lorena only felt more hurt and angry. She went to the bathroom and took a long, hot shower. When she got out, she fixed a cup of coffee and received the morning paper from housekeeping. She sat at the table in her room and read.

When she saw the article on Mark, she nearly spit out her coffee. Lorena had a feeling that he was attacked because of his involvement with her. She couldn't quite figure out who it was or how, but she was terrified it was her fault. Lorena couldn't stop wondering what Phillip would say when he got back. What if they brought her in for questioning? What would she say? Would she lie to them to cover her ass with Chad or would she come clean? Lorena didn't know.

Thinking Chad was probably long gone by then, she risked seeing him when she went down to the hot tub. Lorena sat in the tub alone with her eyes closed. She went over the past month or so in great detail trying to figure out what she felt and what she wanted. Had an entire month gone by already? It seemed like it was only yesterday she'd gotten herself into this huge mess. Lorena thought about the freedom she felt with Phillip and the obligations she felt where Chad was concerned. At the end of her time soaking, she decided to say screw Chad and take off for Japan. She'd sort it all out later after she knew how Chad was going to react to her leaving. Lorena got out of the tub and dried off. She went back up to her room, put on a nice dress and treated herself to breakfast at the restaurant across the street.

After breakfast, Lorena went up to her hotel room and phoned the airport. She found an airline that could book her a ticket to Tokyo that day. She was extremely excited when she called Phillip at his hotel to tell him her plans. Phillip was ecstatic to hear from her. He'd already heard about Mark and was deeply concerned about his friend. So much so that he was planning to come back a little early. He apologized to Lorena about not being able to spend more time together, but he felt it was best under the circumstances.

"I'm disappointed, but I understand," a saddened Lorena said.

"I'm here now darling. How 'bout some phone sex?"

"I've never been one to talk dirty."

"Well now is a good time to start." He laughed.

After both of them had cum, they hung up. Lorena slipped back into her hotel bed wet, warm and ecstatic. Why hadn't she let herself be wilder in high school and college? She didn't feel bad being a naughty girl in the least bit. In truth, she was rather enjoying it.

CHAPTER 10

The next day Lorena checked out of the hotel and went to the airport. She was going to book a ticket to Tokyo, anyway, even if Phillip wasn't going to be there. But when she arrived at the ticket counter she discovered all of her credit and debit cards had been reported as stolen and canceled. Lorena couldn't fathom Chad stooping so low, but it appeared as if he had. Distraught and angry, she realized she didn't even have enough cash for a cab ride home. She decided to call her friend Nikki, collect.

"Nikki, it's me Lorena."

"What's going on?

"A lot. I was going to go take off for Japan, but all my credit cards were canceled and I don't have enough cash for a cab. Could you come and get me?"

"Wow, really?" Nikki paused, shocked and then said, "What happened."

"Nikki, I'll explain all that later. Can you please just hurry?"

"Sure, no problem. Wait for me in front. I'll be there in twenty."

They disconnected and Lorena traipsed to the front of the airport. She was disappointed she couldn't leave and more than a little angry to think Chad had done this on purpose. She didn't have long stew over it before for Nikki arrived in her black Porsche. Lorena threw her bags in the back seat, climbed in the passenger seat and closed her eyes.

As the pulled away, Nikki said "What flight were you supposed to be on?"

"Flight Eight-Fifteen to Tokyo, Japan."

"That's too bad. Maybe we get can some things straightened around get you on another flight."

"Thank you," Lorena said with a sad smile.

At ten that night, Lorena arrived home with her bags in tow. The house was dark and Chad was nowhere to be found. She unpacked and called Phillip. He wasn't at the hotel, so she tried his cell phone. He was laid over in Hawaii, but he was on his way back to California.

It didn't occur to her until after she hung up that her phone calls to Phillip could show up on the phone bill and Chad might use that against her. She scolded herself for not being more discreet. She lay there for a while, thinking of Phillip and fearing Chad before she drifted off to sleep.

***

Late that night Phillip got back to the States. When he checked his voice mail on his cell phone he heard an urgent message from Lorena asking him to rush back to her house. He tried to call her, but there was no answer. He decided to swing by her house before heading home just in case there was some sort of emergency.

Phillip used his key fob to disarm the alarm for his car. In the dark, he searched for the handle, found it and was going to get in before a crowbar hit him in the head. He crumpled against the car, unable to stand up straight. Phillip tried to turn and see who'd hit him, but all he manage to see was a black ski mask before a fist bashed his face. Phillip was sliding down the car when the assailant picked him up and hit him again. Phillip couldn't collect himself enough to fight back. He was barely conscious as the attacker let him fall to the ground and he was kicked repeatedly in the stomach. Phillip cried out as his ribs suffered the brunt of the blows. They cracked and broke. His nose and mouth were bleeding and teeth were dislodged, popping out of his mouth as he gagged and spit. The intense pain was soon replaced with numbness. The attacker took off, apparently leaving Phillip for dead.

Phillip died an hour later before anyone found him.

***

Chad arrived home at midnight. He took a shower to wash off the blood and sweat before he collapsed into bed beside his wife. Lorena stirred ever so slightly when he rolled in beside her. Although he didn't touch her and they didn't speak, Lorena sensed something was dreadfully wrong.

The next morning Lorena rose and tried to call Phillip while Chad ran on the treadmill. He never ran on the treadmill, so doing it now was strange, but at least it gave Lorena a few moments to herself. She received no answer and grew increasingly worried about her friend and lover. Chad got off the treadmill and ate some breakfast with Lorena. He ate his bagel and cream cheese as he read the paper, saying nothing. Lorena drank her coffee, wondering where he'd been all night and if he had anything to do with Phillip suddenly going MIA.

Suddenly, Chad put the paper down and smiled at his solemn wife. "Why don't we go back upstairs and sleep in a bit."

Lorena was bewildered by this request, considering he'd just satisfied his uncontrollable urges with the redhead at the hotel. Was it possible Chad had done something bad to Mark and Phillip and was more turned on by that then her? She shuddered inwardly and then said as calmly as she could, "Nah, I have work in less than a half an hour. They've missed me at the gallery this week while I was away."

Chad didn't miss a beat. He smiled coyly. "We have time for a quickie."

"I really can't be late today. Maybe when I get home though we can have all the fun you want." She gave him a fake smile to go with the lie.

He leaned forward, insistent. "I don't want to wait."

"But waiting makes it so much better. The anticipation is a turn-on in itself."

Chad kissed her, but she eased him away and went upstairs, taking the paper with her. Lorena got dressed and went to work as usual. At work, the dull, boring routine was a relief from the tension and anxiety at home. But then she heard about the murder at the airport. Everyone was talking about it. Lorena turned the TV on in the break room to see the breaking story.

The man who was murdered was identified as millionaire Phillip Eszterhas.

Lorena felt like someone had driven a stake into her stomach as they showed his picture and talked about how he'd been beaten to death in the airport parking lot. Security tapes showed a man dressed in black and wearing a ski mask doing the beating, which was brutal to watch. Lorena was thankful none of the news stations aired more than a clip of the tape, which the newscaster said was fifteen minutes long. She sat in a chair and tried not let tears escape her eyes.

"Who would do such a thing," one of her co-workers asked from behind her.

She shook her head like she didn't know, but the truth was she did have a pretty good idea who it could be. She was afraid it had been Chad. She always knew he was capable of terrible violence even though she'd never seen it firsthand. She had been able to sense the tenseness and darkness in his heart. He was not only cold hearted, he was psychotic. She trembled with fear, not wanting to go back home to face him that night.

Lorena muted the TV volume and went to the phone on the wall. She called her friend Nikki.

"Did you see the story about Phillip on TV?"

"No. Why? What happened?"

"He was killed last night at the airport. He'd just gotten in from Japan."

"No, *that's terrible.* Who did it? Do the police have any suspects?"

"I don't think so, but I have some ideas. Look, can we meet and talk about this after work? I don't think it's safe for me."

"Why do you think you're in danger? Think you might be next?"

"Uh-huh."

"Come to my office after you get off work. We'll talk then."

Lorena agreed, placed the phone back on its cradle and lifted it up for a new dial tone. She called a client and arranged to see him another day. She couldn't handle going about her business as normal when her world was falling apart. Lorena was scared. Without Phillip, she didn't know who else to turn to besides her friend Nikki.

Nikki's office was modernistic and sleek looking, but there were homey touches. Soft music played in the waiting room. The colors were warm and inviting. The receptionist who greeted Lorena was friendly and helpful.

"I'm here to see Doctor Nikki Stone. I'm a friend."

"Let me call her," she said, and did.

After a few minutes Lorena was standing in her friend's office. Nikki came up to her and gave her a huge hug. "I'm so glad to see you. Are you all right, hon?"

Lorena nodded and slumped on Nikki's black leather couch. "I'm just so scared. I don't know what to do."

"Why?"

"Someone is after me. Philip's death is all my fault," she cried.

"How could it be your fault? You didn't send out a hit man to kill him and you certainly didn't kill him yourself."

"No, but I cheated on my husband by sleeping with Phillip. If I hadn't of cheated on Chad none of this would have happened. I'm such a horrible person."

"Why, do you think his death is a sort punishment? Who's punishing you?"

Lorena was visibly shaken, but her eyes had remained dry until that moment. Tears welled up and threatened to spill over. "I don't know!"

"I think you know who's after you, but you're afraid to say it."

"I pissed someone off is all." Lorena wagged her hand in the air three times while she said, "Mark, Phillip, Dad."

Nikki's eyebrows knitted, "Dad? You mean *Chad*?"

Lorena nodded.

***

Nikki started to put two and two together and think Dad and Chad were connected. Nikki's profession allowed her to assemble the pieces of the puzzle of her friend's psyche. Lorena had married a man exactly like her dad and he must have been angry and abusive. Most abuse is subtle enough, but occasionally the victimizer can have a psychotic break and become homicidal. Did Chad's jealousy of Lorena's affairs cause him to snap, she wondered? Nikki began to formulate how to deal with this crisis. She touched Lorena's arm and said gently, "Why don't you stay at my house tonight. You'll be safe there. We'll deal with the rest later."

"Chad will just get even madder at me and God knows what he'll do next. He might even come after you for helping me."

"You let me handle Chad."

So it was settled. Nikki finished up some paper work and drove Lorena back to her apartment. Nikki's home was more old-fashioned and cluttered than her office. The difference between her home and office seemed to reflect a person who had two personalities. Nikki fixed herself and Lorena cups of Sweet Dreams tea and they talked for a long time before going to sleep. Lorena dozed on the couch and Nikki finally got out of her chair and went to her bedroom around midnight.

From her bedroom, Nikki called Chad at home. "Chad?" she said when he answered.

"Yes," he answered, anger spilling out in his tone.

"This is Nikki, Lorena's friend."

"Where the fuck is my wife?"

Nikki could see why Lorena was afraid. "Here. She and I were talking for a long time. You know how we girls can gab. Anyway, she wasn't feeling well and I told her she could sleep here tonight. She fell asleep before she could call you. I thought I'd call so you wouldn't be worried."

"How wonderfully nice," he said, sarcasm dripping from his mouth. "Now put my wife on."

"No, I told you she wasn't feeling well and was asleep. I am not waking her up."

"Damn it! Don't you be covering for her. I know she's cheating on me."

"I don't know anything about that. I told you she was ill and you have no reason not to believe me. I don't appreciate your tone." Nikki understood why Lorena had such a difficult time dealing with her formable husband. He was going off on everyone and his rage wasn't focused any one particular person or thing. He was going to explode like a bomb and she had to make sure Lorena wasn't around when it happened, or at least not alone when it happened.

"I saw her," Chad continued. "I saw her fucking Amber. Did you fuck her, too?"

"I have never done any such thing and even if I did, it wouldn't be any of your business."

He continued on raving so Nikki hung up on him. There was no talking to him or getting through to him when he was that inflamed. Nikki crawled into bed, wanting to be blot out her pain and her fears.

Nikki was distressed by the call. She thrashed about in the bed, hoping Chad didn't do something violent and stupid before they could stop him. Her sleep was sparse that night and in the morning she exhorted that Lorena to go to a battered women's shelter.

Lorena said, "But he's never once hit me. How can I be a battered woman if he's never beaten me or raised a hand to me?"

She had a point, but Nikki was adamant. "There is a first time for everything."

"This is ridiculous. I can't believe I even considered that Chad would do something so crazy."

"You know what he's capable of. Why are you pretending nothing has happened?"

"Look, I'm not going to listen to this. I've got to get to work." With that, Lorena shut Nikki's bathroom door with a slam.

When Lorena came out of the bathroom, Nikki was waiting there for her. "Please reconsider."

"Thank you, but I need to get going to work. Okay?" She pulled open Nikki's apartment door and fled, leaving Nikki to wonder why Lorena was in such denial over what she knew to be true. Why couldn't she see what was right in front of her eyes? Lorena was in danger.

CHAPTER 11

Nikki yanked her shoes on and started to follow her, but then she stopped. She saw Chad coming down the hall.

"Where is she?" he yelled, knowing that Lorena had already left. He wanted to make sure Nikki was alone. "Where is Lorena," he said again.

Nikki was defensive, angry and afraid, "She isn't here, so leave! Leave before I call the cops."

Chad gazed around the apartment, putting on a show as if searching to see if he could see his wife. He stopped looking around and looked directly as Nikki. "*Don't* you ever fuck with my wife or put any of those goddamn ideas in her head again. You stay away from her. You hear?"

"I'm sorry Chad, but I can't stay away. She needs me. I know what you've done to her. You've lied and cheated on her countless times. She knows about your redheaded friend at the Sherida—"

Chad backhanded with a blow her across the face. Nikki touched her hand to her throbbing red cheek. It hurt like hell.

Nikki glared at him thinking of how nice it would feel to kick his pompous ass, but she retrained herself. "I don't have to take this from you. Get out now or I'll call the cops!"

"No, I don't think so. I think you don't have a choice," he said grasping her arm. "If my wife can fuck you, so can I."

Frightened, Nikki yelled, "Lorena and I have *not* slept together. We are old friends from high school and nothing more. Why can't you get that through your thick skull?"

Chad let go of her arm to swing a right hook and hit her. Both stunned and hurt, Nikki fell to the floor. Chad stepped inside, slammed the door shut behind him and leaned down. He pinned Nikki to the floor, but Nikki kept struggling against him. Chad hit her once again, bloodying her nose and lip. Nikki wiped the blood off with the back of her hand as Chad made a move to unzip his pants. Terrified of what was about to happen, Nikki kneed him in the crotch. He rolled over off of her in a great deal of pain; Nikki jumped up and ran to the phone. Chad had apparently had enough fun and knew he was about to get himself into deep trouble because he pulled himself up and ran out the door before Nikki had dialed 911.

Still holding the cordless phone in her hand, Nikki collapsed onto her couch. She knew she had to make a report to the police, but feared it would be too late by then. She knew she had to find and protect Lorena at all costs. She cleaned herself up and rushed over to the museum to try and talk some sense into her friend. When she arrived, there was no Lorena. Linda told her that Lorena hadn't shown up for work. It was so unlike her to skip work. She asked to see Lorena's desk and Linda let her. Nikki couldn't find any sort of clues or anything to help her. She decided Lorena must have gone home, which was the worst place for her to go. Chad would kill her for sure if she returned home.

In a panic, Nikki raced in her Porsche directly to Lorena and Chad's house.

CHAPTER 12

Lorena had gone to see Mark who she thought was still at Phillip's house. Phillip's part-time maid opened the door after Lorena rang the bell. The maid said Mark had returned home, but she didn't know where his home was. Lorena was frustrated and bewildered. She didn't even know Mark's last name to look him up. Tired and unsure of what to do next, Lorena decided to head home. She hoped and prayed she could go to bed without Chad yelling at her or molesting her. Lorena wanted nothing more than to be left alone.

The drive back to her house was quiet and uneventful. When she arrived at her house, the doors were unlocked, but no one appeared to be home. With a sigh of relief, Lorena went upstairs and lay on the bed fully clothed. She was half asleep when she heard someone come inside the house. It had to be Chad. She remained still even as he barged into the room like an angry bull.

"There you are? Where the hell have you been," he thundered.

Lorena's eyes popped open and she sat up. "What? Huh? Oh, I was at a friend's house. I didn't feel well, so I thought I'd come to rest instead of going to work. I need to call work and let them know I won't be in today."

"I'm tired of your lies."

"Lies? What about all your lies?"

He slapped her across the face. "Don't you ever talk to me like that again!"

"Why? Because all I am is your worthless whore?"

He jabbed his finger in her face. "Why do you do this to me? Why do you make me so angry at you?"

"Oh, so everything is my fault now?" she said her voice shaky with emotion.

"If you weren't such a tight-assed bitch…"

"What? You'd what? You'd still go around fucking all those women because you can. Just because I won't do everything they will is no reason to betray me."

"Oh, like you are so innocent yourself!" His voice got louder with each remark made. He crossed his arms and eyed her with a menacing glare.

"I would have never cheated on you if you had respected me more."

"Excuses, excuses, excuses. You loved fucking those two men and that woman. I just want to know why you didn't tell me. We could have done those things together! I'm open to new things you know."

"Like hell you are. Why do you think I excluded you? Because I was angry with you for the exact same thing that you're bitching at me for." One for Lorena, she thought proudly to herself.

"That's not the point."

"Then what is?"

"You betrayed me. You lied to me and cheated on me. I'm the victim here, not you."

Lorena couldn't help herself. She laughed. How could Chad be so stupid as to not hear what he said? Her laughter enraged him all the more. He backhanded her and she fell to the side of the bed, now becoming livid.

"I can't believe you did that!" she cried, pulling herself up.

"It was long overdue," Chad said climbing on the bed. He grabbed her, threw her prone on the bed and climbed on top of her. "And it's about time you showed me this new side of you. I'm your husband after all."

"No! Get off of me!" She struggled beneath him.

"You're only going to make this harder on yourself."

Lorena felt like weeping. Who was this man? This angry monster was not the man she'd married. The very fact that he'd changed before her eyes scared her as much as the outright violence did. "Chad," she protested. But he didn't listen. She eventually stopped struggling. It's pointless, she thought.

Lorena heard the door open and a loud noise. A moment later a familiar voice called out, "Lorena! Lorena, are you home?"

"Nikki! I'm up here!" she cried out before Chad could stop her. Right after she shouted, he crushed his lips against hers.

Nikki found her way up to the bedroom. Once inside the doorway she yelled, "It's over."

Chad rolled off of Lorena and rolled his eyes. "Oh God, not you. I should've shut you up for good when I had the chance."

Lorena sat up as Chad jumped off the bed and approached Nikki. "I suggest you leave. This is private property and what goes on between me and my wife is private. Get it?" He jabbed a forefinger at her. "You do not belong here. Butt out."

"I can't let you beat and rape her."

"How dare you accuse me of such at thing? If you know what's good for you, you'll turn around and leave here and never come back. Oh swear to God I'll—"

"Or you'll what?" Nikki said jetting out her chin and squaring her stance. "You'll kill me like you did Phillip?"

A gasp came from Lorena who hadn't wanted to admit to herself what she already knew. After a moment of silence, she asked, "Why?"

Chad turned to his wife. "Because he touched you. He took you. He made you his little whore. You were so pure and innocent before Phillip corrupted you."

"Like all those women that you sleep with?"

"That's enough!"

"Why? I mean how could you kill someone? How could you be so cold blooded and cruel? Where did your morals go? Your heart? Your soul?"

"I had an urge, an uncontrollable urge. Would you rather I killed you instead? I couldn't stand by and let this happen. I had to do something. I was so … angry."

Nikki snorted, "You were so weak. You felt out of control and have constantly tried to get it back. Well it's too late. You just bought yourself a one-way ticket to a life sentence in prison."

"Oh, I don't think so. Who'd ever believe you? No one has made any connections between Phillip and Lorena. And I will be long gone before anyone will be able to prove anything." He stepped back, seized Lorena's hand and pulled her off the bed.

"No," she said, shaking her hand free. "I'm not going anywhere with you."

He grasped her arm again and shook her. "Now."

A policeman stepped out of the hallway and into the doorway. "You aren't going anywhere."

The look of shock on Chad's face was priceless. Lorena was delighted to see the look of panic wash over him. The policeman handcuffed Chad as he recited the Miranda rights. He was led downstairs and to the police cruiser. Lorena stood in the doorway as he turned, looked back at Lorena and shot her a look that, if it had it been a weapon, would have been a flame thrower aimed to kill.

Another police officer informed Lorena and Nikki that they needed to go downtown and make an official statement about what had happened. He also gave them the choice whether to go to the hospital first to be checked out, or ride in the squad car. Both women refused to go to the hospital. They went directly downtown to ensure their side of the story was heard in precise detail.

CHAPTER 13

While they were waiting in a tiny interview room at the station, Nikki and Lorena talked about what had just transpired.

"How did you know" Lorena asked Nikki.

"I just had to listen closely. You knew, somewhere deep inside of you, Chad had done it, but because you were so scared and in such denial, I had to take action for you."

"I didn't want to believe I married some capable of such violence. I thought I loved him and I couldn't fathom having married a killer. I guess no one wants to admit they were blind to the truth."

"Nope, besides, you talked about the verbal abuse. When Chad knocked on my door and hit me, it was obvious he was going to try and hurt you next. I saw the fire of anger in his eyes and knew he wouldn't stop until he felt he'd destroyed the source of his discontent. I was scared of Chad, but I also knew I had all the proof I needed."

"So how did you get the cops to come and listen to your little sting operation?" Lorena said, smiling

"I begged and I pleaded. I finally convinced them to meet me at your house and investigate. I promised them it would be worth their time that there was definitely a domestic dispute and possibly an attempt at murder going down. They wanted to barge in and stop any violence immediately, but I told them they could get enough info to put this man away for life if they hung out in the shadows waiting for a full confession."

"What made you think that Chad would confess?"

Nikki pointed to her bruised jaw. "He confessed as he hit me. He can't seem to control himself once the rage is released. I knew he wouldn't be able to keep calm enough to lie when he was in such a state."

"I'm glad you didn't listen to me. I'm sorry I was so stubborn about the whole thing."

"Just doing my job … as your friend." Nikki smiled.

"Thanks for everything." They hugged, but carefully as both were sore from fighting with Chad.

An officer came in with a detective and they related their stories to him in great detail. Chad was charged with domestic violence, assault and battery, attempted rape and murder. Things looked excellent for Lorena and condemning for her husband.

Chad didn't remain her husband for long. During the long waiting period before his trial could begin, she had divorce papers served to him in jail. When the case did go to trial, some of the charges were dropped, but he still managed to end up with twenty years to life in prison for murder. There was, unfortunately, a possibility of parole for good behavior after the twenty years passed. His money and his connections kept him from getting life or the death penalty.

***

The night after he was arrested, Lorena returned to her empty estate and wept. She cried long and hard before she decided to sell the house and most of the things inside of it. She didn't want anything to remind her of her old life. Lorena moved away from her old home in Big Sur and bought a tiny house in the mountains of Colorado.

Nikki moved with her to Colorado and became her roommate. After many wild adventures together, they eventually settled down and had a child together via invitro. Lorena got to carry and give birth to the child she'd always longed for. The violence and darkness of the past was but a faded memory.

About the Author

Cari Lynn Vaughn is the author of three previous collections of poetry and one collection of short stories.

Although she has never solved any mysteries in real life, she did get her start writing as in intern at age 13 for her local newspaper The Daily Globe in Shelby, Ohio. She was also robbed at gunpoint while working at M&S Pizza and Carryout, but was never taken hostage. Currently, she is lives with her two children and is at work on her next novel

ALL THINGS THAT MATTER PRESS, Inc. ™

FOR MORE INFORMATION ON TITLES AVAILABLE FROM
ALL THINGS THAT MATTER PRESS, GO TO
http://allthingsthatmatterpress.com
or contact us at
allthingsthatmatterpress@gmail.com

www.ingramcontent.com/pod-product-compliance
Lightning Source LLC
Chambersburg PA
CBHW051139260626
47170CB00005B/1887